Theodore Boone
# THE ABDUCTION

# John
# Grisham

## Theodore Boone
# THE ABDUCTION

HODDER &
STOUGHTON

First published in Great Britain in 2011 by Hodder & Stoughton
An Hachette UK company

1

Copyright © Belfry Holdings, Inc., 2011

The right of John Grisham to be identified as the Author
of the Work has been asserted by him in accordance
with the Copyright, Designs and Patents Act 1988.

A CIP catalogue record for this title is available from the British Library

ISBN 978 1 444 71453 1

Printed and bound by Clays Ltd, St Ives plc

Hodder & Stoughton policy is to use papers that are natural, renewable and
recyclable products and made from wood grown in sustainable forests. The logging
and manufacturing processes are expected to conform to the environmental
regulations of the country of origin.

Hodder & Stoughton Ltd
338 Euston Road
London NW1 3BH

www.hodder.co.uk

# Chapter 1

The abduction of April Finnemore took place in the dead of night, sometime between 9:15 p.m., when she last spoke with Theo Boone, and 3:30 a.m., when her mother entered her bedroom and realized she was gone. The abduction appeared to have been rushed; whoever took April did not allow her to gather her things. Her laptop was left behind. Though her bedroom was fairly neat, there was some clothing strewn about, which made it difficult to determine if she had been able to pack. Probably not, the police thought. Her toothbrush was still by the sink. Her backpack was by her bed. Her pajamas were on the floor, so she at least had been allowed to change. Her mother, when she wasn't crying or ranting, told the police that her daughter's favorite blue-and-white sweater was not in the closet. And April's favorite sneakers were gone, too.

The police soon dismissed the notion that she'd simply run away. There was no reason to run away, her mother assured them, and she had not packed the things that would make such an escape successful.

A quick inspection of the home revealed no apparent break-in. The windows were all closed and locked, as were the three doors downstairs. Whoever took April was careful enough to close the door behind them, and lock it on the way out. After observing the scene and listening to Mrs. Finnemore for about an hour, the police decided to have a talk with Theo Boone. He was, after all, April's best friend, and they usually chatted by phone or online at night before going to sleep.

At the Boone home, the phone rang at 4:33, according to the digital clock next to the bed where the parents slept. Mr. Woods Boone, the lighter sleeper, grabbed the phone, while Mrs. Marcella Boone rolled over and began wondering who would call at such an hour. When Mr. Boone said, "Yes, Officer," Mrs. Boone really woke up and scrambled out of bed. She listened to his end of the conversation, soon understood that it had something to do with April Finnemore, and was really confused when her husband said, "Sure, Officer, we can be over there in fifteen minutes." He hung up, and she said, "What is it, Woods?"

"Apparently, April's been abducted, and the police would like to talk to Theo."

"I doubt if he abducted her."

"Well, if he's not upstairs in his room, we may have a problem."

He was upstairs in his room, sound asleep, undisturbed by the ringing of the phone. As he threw on blue jeans and a sweatshirt, he explained to his parents that he had called April the night before on his cell phone and they'd chatted for a few minutes, same as usual.

As they drove through Strattenburg in the predawn darkness, Theo could think of nothing but April and of her miserable home life, her warring parents, her scarred brother and sister, both of whom had fled as soon as they were old enough. April was the youngest of three children born to two people who had no business having a family. Both parents were crazy, according to April herself, and Theo certainly agreed. Both had drug convictions. Her mother kept goats on a small farm outside of town and made cheese, bad cheese in Theo's opinion. She peddled it around town in an old funeral hearse painted yellow, with a pet spider monkey riding shotgun. Her father was an aging hippie, who still played in a bad garage band with a bunch of other leftovers from the 1980s. He had no real job and was often gone for weeks. The Finnemores were in a perpetual state of separation, with talk of divorce always in the air.

April confided in Theo, and told him things he vowed to never repeat.

The Finnemore home was owned by someone else, a rental house April hated because her parents had no interest in maintaining it. It was in an older section of Strattenburg, on a shady street lined with other postwar homes that had seen better days. Theo had been there only one time, for a less-than-successful birthday party April's mother had thrown together two years earlier. Most of the kids who'd been invited did not attend because their parents wouldn't allow it. Such was the Finnemore family reputation.

There were two police cars in the driveway when the Boones arrived. Across the street, the neighbors were on their porches, watching.

Mrs. Finnemore—she went by the name of May and had named her children April, March, and August—was in the living room on a sofa talking to a uniformed officer when the Boones entered, rather awkwardly. Quick introductions were made; Mr. Boone had never met her.

"Theo!" Mrs. Finnemore said, very dramatically. "Someone has taken our April!" Then she burst into tears and reached to hug Theo. He wanted no part of being hugged but went along with the ritual out of respect. As always, she wore a large flowing garment that was more of a tent than a dress, light brown in color and made from what appeared to be burlap. Her long graying hair was pulled into a tight ponytail. Crazy as she was, Theo had always been struck by her beauty. She made no effort at being attractive—quite unlike his mother—but some things you can't hide. She was also very creative, liked to paint and do pottery, in addition to making goat cheese. April had inherited the good genes— the pretty eyes, the artistic flair.

When Mrs. Finnemore settled down, Mrs. Boone asked the officer, "What happened?" He responded with a quick summary of what little they knew at that point.

"Did you talk to her last night?" the officer asked Theo. The cop's name was Bolick, Sergeant Bolick, which Theo knew because he'd seen him around the courthouse. Theo knew most of the policemen in Strattenburg, as well as most of the lawyers, judges, janitors, and clerks in the courthouse.

"Yes, sir. At nine fifteen, according to my phone log. We talk almost every night before going to bed," Theo said. Bolick had the reputation of being a wise guy. Theo wasn't prepared to like him.

"How sweet. Did she say anything that might be useful here? Was she worried? Scared?"

Theo was immediately caught in a vise. He could not

lie to a police officer, yet he could not tell a secret that he'd promised he wouldn't tell. So he fudged a bit by saying, "I don't recall anything like that." Mrs. Finnemore was no longer crying; she was staring intensely at Theo, her eyes glowing.

"What did you talk about?" Sergeant Bolick asked. A detective in plainclothes entered the room and listened carefully.

"The usual stuff. School, homework, I don't remember everything." Theo had watched enough trials to know that answers should often be kept vague, and that "I don't recall" and "I don't remember" were perfectly acceptable in many instances.

"Did you chat online?" the detective asked.

"No, sir, not last night. Just phone." They often used Facebook and text messages, but Theo knew not to volunteer information. Just answer the question in front of you. He'd heard his mother say this to her clients many times.

"Any sign of a break-in?" Mr. Boone asked.

"None," said Bolick. "Mrs. Finnemore was sound asleep in the downstairs bedroom, she heard nothing, and at some point she got up to check on April. That's when she realized she was gone."

Theo looked at Mrs. Finnemore, who again shot him a

fierce look. He knew the truth, and she knew he knew the truth. Trouble was, Theo couldn't tell the truth because he'd made a promise to April.

The truth was that Mrs. Finnemore had not been home for the past two nights. April had been living alone, terrified, with all the doors and windows locked as tightly as possible; with a chair jammed against her bedroom door; with an old baseball bat across the end of her bed; with the phone close and ready to dial 911, and with no one in the world to talk to but Theodore Boone, who had vowed not to tell a soul. Her father was out of town with his band. Her mother was taking pills and losing her mind.

"In the past few days, has April said anything about running away?" the detective was asking Theo.

Oh, yes. Nonstop. She wants to run away to Paris and study art. She wants to run away to LA and live with March, her older sister. She wants to run away to Santa Fe and become a painter. She wants to run away, period.

"I don't recall anything like that," Theo said, and it was the truth because "in the past few days" could mean almost anything; thus, the question was too vague to require a definite answer on his part. He had seen this time and time again in trials. In his opinion, Sergeant Bolick and the detective were being far too sloppy with their questions. So far, they had not been able to pin him down, and he had not told a lie.

May Finnemore was overcome with tears and made a big show out of crying. Bolick and the detective quizzed Theo about April's other friends, any potential problems she was having, how she was doing in school, and so on. Theo gave straight answers, with no wasted words.

A female officer in uniform had entered the den from upstairs, and she sat with Mrs. Finnemore, who was again distraught and overcome. Sergeant Bolick nodded at the Boones and motioned for them to follow him into the kitchen. They did, and the detective joined them. Bolick glared at Theo and in a low voice said, "Did the girl ever mention a relative in prison in California?"

"No, sir," Theo said.

"Are you sure?"

"Sure I'm sure."

"What's this all about?" Mrs. Boone jumped in. She was not about to stand by silently while her son was rudely interrogated. Mr. Boone was ready to pounce, too.

The detective pulled out an 8" x 10" black-and-white photo, a mug shot of a shady-looking character who gave every indication of being a veteran criminal. Bolick went on, "Guy's name is Jack Leeper, a ten-time loser. Distant cousin to May Finnemore, even more distant to April. He grew up around here, drifted away a long time ago, became a career thug, petty thief, drug dealer, and so on. Got busted in California for kidnapping ten years ago, sentenced to life with no parole. Escaped two weeks ago. This afternoon we get a tip that he might be in this area."

Theo looked at the sinister face of Jack Leeper and felt ill. If this thug had April, then she was in serious trouble.

Bolick continued, "Last night around seven thirty, Leeper here walks into the Korean Quick Shop four blocks away, buys cigarettes and beer, gets his face captured on the surveillance cameras. Not the smartest crook in the world. So, we know he's definitely in the area."

"Why would he take April?" Theo blurted, his mouth dry with fear, his knees ready to buckle.

"According to authorities in California, they found some letters from April in his prison cell. She was his pen pal, probably felt sorry for the guy 'cause he's never supposed to get out of prison. So she strikes up a correspondence. We've searched her room upstairs and can't find anything he may have written to her."

"She never mentioned this to you?" the detective asked.

"Never," Theo said. He had learned that with April's weird family there were many secrets, many things she kept to herself.

The detective put away the photo, and Theo was relieved.

He never wanted to see the face again, but he doubted if he could ever forget it.

Sergeant Bolick said, "We suspect that April knew the person who took her. How else can you explain the lack of a forcible entry?"

"Do you think he would hurt her?" Theo asked.

"We have no way of knowing that, Theo. This man's been in prison most of his life. His behavior is unpredictable."

The detective added, "The good thing is that he always gets caught."

Theo said, "If April's with him, she'll contact us. She'll find a way."

"Then, please let us know."

"Don't worry."

"Excuse me, Officer," Mrs. Boone said. "But I thought in a case like this you first investigate the parents. Missing children are almost always taken by one of their parents, right?"

"This is correct," Bolick said. "And we are looking for the father. According to the mother, though, she spoke with him yesterday afternoon and he was with his band somewhere in West Virginia. She feels rather strongly that he is not involved in this."

"April can't stand her father," Theo blurted, then wished he'd remained quiet.

They chatted for a few more minutes, but the conversation was obviously over. The officers thanked the Boones for coming and promised to check back later. Both Mr. and Mrs. Boone said they would be at their office all day if they were needed for anything. Theo, of course, would be in school.

As they drove away, Mrs. Boone said, "That poor child. Snatched from her own bedroom."

Mr. Boone, who was driving, glanced back over his shoulder and said, "Are you okay, Theo?"

"I guess," he said.

"Of course he's not okay, Woods. His friend has just been abducted."

"I can speak for myself, Mom," Theo said.

"Of course you can, dear. I just hope they find her, and soon."

There was a hint of sunlight to the east. As they drove through the residential neighborhood, Theo stared out of his window, searching for the hardened face of Jack Leeper. But no one was out there. Lights in homes were being turned on. The town was waking up.

"It's almost six," Mr. Boone announced. "I say we go to Gertrude's and have her world-famous waffles. Theo?"

"I'm in," Theo replied, though he had no appetite.

"Marvelous, honey," Mrs. Boone said, though all three knew she would have nothing but coffee.

Gertrude's was an old diner on Main Street, six blocks west of the courthouse and three blocks south of the police station. It claimed to serve pecan waffles that were famous around the world, but Theo had often doubted this. Did people in Japan and Greece really know about Gertrude and her waffles? He wasn't so sure. He had friends at school who'd never heard of Gertrude's right there in Strattenburg. A few miles west of town, on the main highway, there was an ancient log cabin with a gas pump out front and a large sign advertising Dudley's World-Famous Mint Fudge. When Theo was younger, he naturally had assumed that everybody in town not only craved the mint fudge but talked about it nonstop. How else could it achieve the status of being world famous? Then one day in class the discussion took an odd turn and found its way to the topic of imports and exports. Theo made the observation that Mr. Dudley and his mint fudge were heavy into exports because they were so famous. It said so right there on the billboard. To his astonishment, only one other classmate had ever heard of this fudge. Slowly, Theo realized that it probably was not as well known as Mr. Dudley claimed it to be. Slowly, he began to grasp the concept of false advertising.

Since then, he'd been very suspicious of such big claims of notoriety.

But on this morning he couldn't dwell on waffles and fudge, famous or not. He was far too occupied with thoughts of April and the slimy figure of Jack Leeper. The Boones were seated at a small table in the crowded diner. The air was thick with bacon grease and strong coffee, and the hot topic, as Theo realized not long after he sat down, was the abduction of April Finnemore. To their right, four uniformed policemen talked loudly about the possibility that Leeper was close by. To their left, a table of gray-haired men spoke with great authority on several subjects, but seemed particularly interested in the "kidnapping," as it was sometimes referred to.

The menu promoted the myth that Gertrude's was indeed the home of "World-Famous Pecan Waffles." In silent protest against false advertising, Theo ordered scrambled eggs and sausage. His father ordered waffles. His mother ordered dry wheat toast.

As soon as the waitress walked away, Mrs. Boone looked Theo squarely in the eyes and said, "Okay, let's have it. There's something else to the story."

Theo was constantly amazed at how easily his mother could do this. He could tell only half of a story, and she immediately looked for the other half. He could offer up a little fib, nothing serious, maybe something just for fun, and she instinctively pounced on it and ripped it to shreds. He could duck a direct question, and she would fire back with three more. Theo suspected she had acquired this skill after years as a divorce lawyer. She often said that she never expected her clients to tell her the truth.

"I agree," said Mr. Boone. Theo couldn't tell if he really agreed, or whether he was just tag-teaming with his wife, which he often did. Mr. Boone was a real estate lawyer who never went to court, and, while he missed little, he was usually a step or two behind Mrs. Boone when it came time to grill Theo about something.

"April told me not to tell anyone," Theo said.

To which his mother responded quickly, "And April is in big trouble right now, Theo. If you know something, let's have it. And now." Her eyes narrowed. Her eyebrows arched. Theo knew where this was headed, and, truthfully, he knew it was better to level with his parents.

"Mrs. Finnemore wasn't at home when I talked to April last night," Theo said, his head low, his eyes darting left and right. "And she wasn't home the night before. She's taking pills and she's acting crazy. April's been living by herself."

"Where's her father?" Mr. Boone asked.

"He's off with his band, hasn't been home in a week."

"Doesn't he have a job?" Mrs. Boone asked.

"He buys and sells antique furniture. April says he'll make a few bucks, then disappear for a week or two with his band."

"That poor girl," Mrs. Boone said.

"Are you going to tell the police?" Theo asked.

Both parents took long sips from their coffee cups. They exchanged curious looks as they pondered this. They eventually agreed that they would discuss it later, at the office, while Theo was at school. Mrs. Finnemore was obviously lying to the police, but the Boones were reluctant to get in the middle of that. They doubted if she knew anything about the abduction. She seemed distressed enough. She probably felt guilty for being away when her daughter was taken.

The food arrived and the waitress refilled the coffee cups. Theo was drinking milk.

The situation was very complicated, and Theo was relieved to have his parents involved and doing their share of the worrying.

"Anything else, Theo?" his father asked.

"Not that I can think of."

His mother said, "When you talked to her last night, was she frightened?"

"Yes. She was really scared and also worried about her mother."

"Why didn't you tell us?" his father asked.

"Because she made me promise not to tell. April has to deal with a lot, and she's very private. She's also embarrassed by her family and tries to protect them. She was hoping her mother would show up at any minute. I guess someone else did."

Theo suddenly lost his appetite. He should've done more. He should've tried to protect April by telling his parents or perhaps a teacher at school. Someone would have listened to him. He could have done something. But, April swore him to silence, and she kept assuring him she was safe. The house was locked; plenty of lights were on, and so forth.

During the drive home, Theo said from the rear seat, "I'm not sure I can go to school today."

"I was waiting for that," his father replied.

"What's your reason this time?" his mother said.

"Well, to start with, I didn't get enough sleep last night. We've been up since, what four thirty?"

"So you want to go home and go to sleep?" his father replied.

"I didn't say that, but I doubt if I can stay awake at school."

"I bet you can. Your mother and I are going to work, and we have no choice but to stay awake."

Theo almost blurted something about his father's daily siesta; a brief power nap at the desk with the door locked, usually around 3:00 p.m. Everyone who worked at the law firm of Boone & Boone knew that Woods was upstairs, shoes off, feet on the desk, phone on Do Not Disturb, snoring away for thirty minutes every afternoon.

"You can tough it out," his father added.

Theo's problem at this moment was his habit of trying to avoid school. Headaches, coughs, food poisoning, pulled muscles, stomach gas—Theo had tried them all and would try them again. He didn't hate school; in fact, he usually enjoyed it once he got there. He made good grades and enjoyed his friends. Theo, though, wanted to be at the courthouse, watching trials and hearings, listening to the lawyers and judges, chatting with the policemen and the clerks, even the janitors. Theo knew them all.

"There's another reason I can't go to school," he said, though he knew this was a battle he would not win.

"Let's hear it," his mother said.

"Okay, there's a manhunt underway, and I need to go help. How often do we have a manhunt in Strattenburg? This is a big deal, especially since it's my close friend they're looking for. I need to help search for April. She would expect me to. Plus, there's no way I can concentrate at school. A total waste of time. I'll think of nothing but April."

"Nice try," his father said.

"Not bad," his mother added.

"Look, I'm serious. I need to be on the streets."

"I'm confused," his father said, though he really wasn't. He often claimed to be confused when discussing things with Theo. "You're too tired to go to school, yet you have enough energy to lead a manhunt."

"Whatever. There's no way I can go to school."

———

An hour later, Theo parked his bike outside the middle school and reluctantly went inside as the 8:15 bell was ringing. In the main lobby, he was immediately met by three crying eighth-grade girls who wanted to know if he knew anything about April. He said he knew nothing more than what was being reported on the morning news.

Evidently, everybody in town had watched the morning news. The reports showed a school photo of April, and a mug shot of Jack Leeper. There was a strong suggestion that a kidnapping had taken place. Theo didn't understand this. A kidnapping (and he'd checked the dictionary) usually involved a demand for ransom—cash to be paid for the release of the person seized. The Finnemores couldn't pay their monthly bills—how were they supposed to find serious cash to free April? And there was no word yet from the kidnapper. Usually, as Theo remembered from television, the family gets word pretty soon that the bad guys have the child and would like a million bucks or so for a safe return.

Another report from the morning news showed Mrs. Finnemore crying in front of their home. The police were tight-lipped, saying only that they were pursuing all leads. A neighbor said his dog started barking around midnight, always a bad sign. As frantic as the reporters seemed to be that morning, the truth was that they were finding very little to add to the story of a missing girl.

Theo's homeroom teacher was Mr. Mount, who also taught Government. After Mr. Mount got the boys settled, he called the roll. All sixteen were present. The conversation quickly got around to the disappearance of April, and Mr. Mount asked Theo if he'd heard anything.

"Nothing," Theo said, and his classmates seemed disappointed. Theo was one of the few boys who talked to April. Most of the eighth graders, boys and girls, liked April but found her difficult to hang out with. She was quiet, dressed more like a boy than a girl, had no interest in the latest fashions or the weekly teen-gossip magazines, and as everyone knew, came from a weird family.

The bell rang for first period, and Theo, already exhausted, dragged himself off to Spanish.

# Chapter 3

Final bell rang at 3:30, and by 3:31 Theo was on his bike, speeding away from school, darting through alleys and back streets and dodging downtown traffic. He zipped across Main Street, waved at a policeman standing near an intersection and pretended not to hear when the policeman yelled, "Slow it down, Theo." He cut through a small cemetery and turned onto Park Street.

His parents had been married for twenty-five years, and for the past twenty they had worked together as partners in the small firm of Boone & Boone, located at 415 Park Street, in the heart of old Strattenburg. There had once been another partner, Ike Boone, Theo's uncle, but Ike had been forced to leave the firm when he got himself into some trouble. Now the firm had just two equal partners—Marcella Boone on the first floor, in a neat modern office where she handled mainly divorces, and Woods Boone upstairs all alone in a large cluttered room with sagging bookshelves and stacks of files littering the floor and an ever-present cloud of fragrant pipe smoke rolling gently across the ceiling. Rounding out the firm, there was Elsa, who answered the phone, greeted the clients, managed the office, did some typing, and kept an eye on Judge, the dog; there was Dorothy, a real estate secretary, who worked for Mr. Boone and did work that Theo considered horribly boring; and there was Vince, the paralegal, who worked on Mrs. Boone's cases.

Judge, a mutt who was Theo's dog, the family's dog, and the firm's dog, spent his days at the office, sometimes creeping quietly from room to room keeping an eye on things, oftentimes following a human to the kitchen where he expected food, but mostly snoozing on a small square bed in the reception area where Elsa talked to him whenever she typed.

The last member of the firm was Theo, who happily suspected that he was the only thirteen-year-old in Strattenburg with his own law office. Of course, he was too young to be a real member of the firm, but there were times when Theo was valuable. He fetched files for Dorothy and Vince. He scanned lengthy documents looking for key words or phrases. His computer skills were extraordinary and allowed him to research legal issues and dig up facts. But his favorite chore, by far, was dashing off to the courthouse to file papers for the firm. Theo loved the courthouse and dreamed of the day when he would stand in the large, stately courtroom on the second floor and defend his clients.

At 3:40 p.m., on the dot, Theo parked his bike on the narrow front porch of Boone & Boone, and braced himself. Elsa greeted him every day with a fierce hug, a painful pinch on the check, then a quick inspection of whatever he was wearing. He opened the door, stepped inside, and got himself properly greeted. As always, Judge was waiting, too. He bounced from his bed and ran to see Theo.

"I'm so sorry about April," Elsa gushed. She sounded as if she knew the girl personally, which she did not. But by now, as with any tragedy, everyone in Strattenburg knew or claimed to know April and could say only great things about her.

"Any news?" Theo asked, rubbing Judge's head.

"Nothing. I've listened to the radio all day, no word, no sign of anything. How was school?"

"Terrible. All we did was talk about April."

"That poor girl." Elsa was inspecting his shirt, then her

eyes moved down to his pants and for a split second Theo froze. Every day she looked him over quickly and never hesitated to say something like "Does that shirt really match those pants?" or "Didn't you wear that shirt two days ago?" This irritated Theo tremendously and he had complained to both parents, but nothing came of his protests. Elsa was like a member of the family, a second mother to Theo, and if she wanted to quiz him about anything, she did so out of affection.

The rumor was that Elsa spent all her money on clothes, and she certainly gave that appearance. Apparently, she approved of his attire today. Before she had the chance to comment, Theo kept the conversation going with, "Is my mother in?"

"Yes, but she has a client. Mr. Boone is working."

This was usually the case. Theo's mother, when she wasn't in court, spent most of her time with clients, almost all of whom were women who (1) wanted a divorce, or (2) needed a divorce, or (3) were in the process of getting a divorce, or (4) were suffering through the aftermath of a divorce. It was difficult work, but his mother was known as one of the top divorce lawyers in town. Theo was quite proud of this. He was also proud of the fact that his mother encouraged every new client to seek professional counseling in an effort to save the marriage. Sadly, though, as he'd already learned, some marriages cannot be saved.

He bounced up the stairs with Judge at his heels and barged into the spacious and wonderful office of Woods Boone, Attorney and Counselor-at-Law. His dad was behind his desk, at work, pipe in one hand, pen in the other, with papers scattered everywhere.

"Well, hello, Theo," Mr. Boone said with a warm smile. "A good day at school?" The same question five days a week.

"Terrible," Theo said. "I knew I shouldn't have gone. A total waste."

"And why is that?"

"Come on, Dad. My friend, our classmate, has been snatched by an escaped criminal who was sent to prison because he's a kidnapper. It's not like this happens every day around here. We should've been out there on the streets helping with the manhunt, but no, we were stuck in school where all we did was talk about searching for April."

"Nonsense. Leave the manhunt to the professionals, Theo. We have a fine police force in this city."

"Well, they haven't found her yet. Maybe they need some help."

"Help from whom?"

Theo cleared his throat and clenched his jaw. He stared

straight at his father, and got ready to tell the truth. He'd been taught to confront the truth head-on, hold nothing back, just blurt it all out, and whatever followed would be far better than lying or concealing the truth. He was about to say—"Help from us, Dad, April's friends. I've organized a search party, and we're about to hit the streets"—when the phone rang. His father grabbed it, offered his usual gruff "Woods Boone," then began listening.

Theo held his tongue. After a few seconds, his father covered the receiver and whispered, "This might take a while."

"See you later," Theo said as he jumped to his feet and left. He walked downstairs, Judge following close behind, and made his way to the rear of Boone & Boone, to the small room he called his office. He unloaded his backpack, arranged his books and notebooks, and gave every indication that he was about to plunge into his homework. He was not.

The search party he'd organized consisted of about twenty of his friends. The plan was to hit the streets in five units of four bikes each. They had cell phones and two-way radios. Woody had an iPad with Google Earth and GPS apps. Everything would be coordinated, with Theo, of course, in charge. They would comb certain areas of town searching for April, and they would distribute flyers with her face in the center and the promise of one thousand dollars in reward money for information leading to her rescue. They had passed the hat at school and collected almost two hundred dollars from students and teachers. Theo and his friends figured they could get the rest of the money from their parents in the event someone came forward with crucial information. Surely, Theo had argued, the parents would cough up the money, if necessary. It was risky, but there was so much at stake and so little time.

Theo eased out the back door, leaving Judge alone and confused, then sneaked around to the front and hopped on his bike.

# Chapter 4

The search party came together a few minutes before 4:00 p.m., in Truman Park, the largest park of any kind in the city of Strattenburg. The gang met near the main gazebo, a popular place in the heart of the park, a place where politicians made speeches and bands played on long summer evenings and, occasionally, young couples got married. There were eighteen in all; fifteen boys and three girls, all properly helmeted and eager to find and rescue April Finnemore.

Throughout the day at school, the boys had argued and bickered about how a proper manhunt should be conducted. None had ever taken part in such a search, but this lack of experience was not mentioned or acknowledged.

Instead, several of them, including Theo, spoke as if they knew precisely what to do. Another strong voice belonged to Woody, who, because he owned the iPad, felt as though more weight should be given to his ideas. Another leader was Justin, the best athlete in their class and, therefore, the one with the most self-confidence.

There were skeptics in the eighth grade who believed that Jack Leeper had already fled the area with April. Why would he stay in a place where everyone was looking at his face on television? The skeptics argued that any effort to find her was futile. She was gone, hidden in another state, perhaps another country, hopefully still alive.

But Theo and the others were determined to do something, anything. Maybe she was gone, but maybe she wasn't. No one knew, but at least they were trying. Who knows—they might get lucky.

Late in the day, the searchers finally reached an agreement among themselves. They would concentrate their efforts in an old section known as Delmont, near Stratten College, in the northwest part of the town. Delmont was lower income, with more renters than owners, and popular with students and starving artists. The search party figured any kidnapper worth his salt would stay away from the nicer neighborhoods. He would avoid central Strattenburg with its busy streets and sidewalks. He would almost certainly choose an area where strangers came and went with greater frequency. Thus, they had narrowed their search, and from the moment the decision was made, they were convinced that April was stashed away in a back room of some cheap rental duplex, or perhaps gagged and bound and hidden above an old garage in Delmont.

They split into three teams of six, with a girl included a bit reluctantly to each unit. Ten minutes after they gathered in the park, they wheeled into Gibson's Grocery on the edge of Delmont. Woody's team took Allen Street, Justin's, Edgecomb Street. And Theo, who had assumed the role of supreme commander, though he didn't refer to himself in such a manner, led his team two blocks over to Trover Avenue, where they began tacking MISSING flyers on every utility pole they saw. They stopped at a Laundromat and handed flyers to the people washing their clothes. They chatted with pedestrians on the sidewalks and told them to keep a sharp lookout. They talked to old men rocking on porches and nice ladies pulling weeds from flower beds. They pedaled slowly along Trover, taking in each house, each duplex, each apartment building, and as this went on and on, they began to realize that they were not accomplishing much. If April were locked away inside one of the buildings, how were they supposed to find her? They could not peek in. They could not knock on the door and expect Leeper to answer it. They could not yell at the windows and hope she answered. Theo began to realize that their time was better spent handing out flyers and talking about the reward money.

They finished Trover Avenue and moved a block north to Whitworth Street, where they went door-to-door in a shopping center, passing out flyers in a barbershop, a cleaners, a pizza carryout, and a liquor store. The warning on the door of the liquor store plainly forbade the entry of anyone under the age of twenty-one, but Theo didn't hesitate. He was there to help a friend, not buy booze. He marched inside, alone, handed flyers to the two idle clerks at the cash registers, and walked out before they could protest.

They were leaving the shopping center when an urgent call came from Woody. The police had stopped them on Allen Street, and the police were not happy. Theo and his team took off, and a few minutes later arrived at the scene. There were two city police cars and three uniformed officers.

Theo realized immediately that he did not recognize any of the policemen.

"What are you kids doing here?" the first one asked as Theo approached. His bronze nameplate identified him as Bard. "Lemme guess, you're helping with the search?" Bard said with a sneer.

Theo shoved out his hand and said, "I'm Theo Boone."

He emphasized his last name in hopes that one of the officers might recognize it. He'd learned that most of the policemen knew most of the lawyers, and maybe, just maybe, one of these guys would realize that Theo's parents were well-respected attorneys. But, it didn't work. There were so many lawyers in Strattenburg.

"Yes, sir, we're helping you guys search for April Finnemore," Theo went on pleasantly, flashing his braces with a wide smile at Officer Bard.

"Are you the leader of this gang?" Bard snapped.

Theo glanced at Woody, who'd lost all confidence and appeared frightened, as if he were about to be dragged away to jail and perhaps beaten. "I guess," Theo answered.

"So, who asked you boys and girls to join in the search?"

"Well, sir, no one really asked us. April is our friend and we're worried." Theo was trying to find the right tone. He wanted to be very respectful, but at the same time he was convinced they were doing nothing wrong.

"How sweet," Bard said, grinning at the other two officers. He was holding a flyer and he showed it to Theo. "Who printed these?" he asked.

Theo wanted to say, "Sir, it's really none of your business who printed the flyers." But this would only make a tense situation much worse. So he said, "We printed them at school today."

"And this is April?" Bard said, pointing to the smiling face square in the middle of the flyer.

Theo wanted to say, "No, sir, that's another girl's face we're using to make the search even more difficult by confusing everybody."

April's face had been all over the local news. Surely, Bard recognized her.

Theo said, simply, "Yes, sir."

"And who gave you kids permission to tack these flyers on public property?"

"No one."

"You know it's a violation of city code, against the law? You know this?" Bard had been watching too many bad-cop shows on television, and he was working much too hard to try to frighten the kids.

Justin and his team made a silent entry into the fray. They rolled to a stop behind the other bikers. Eighteen kids, three policemen, and several neighbors drifting over to check on things.

At this point Theo should've played along and professed ignorance of the city's laws, but he simply could not do so. He said, very respectfully, "No, sir, it's not a violation of the city code to put flyers on poles used for telephones and electricity. I checked the law online during school today."

It was immediately obvious that Officer Bard wasn't sure what to say next. His bluff had been called. He glanced at his two pals, both of whom seemed to be amused and not the least bit supportive. The kids were smirking at him. It was Bard against everyone.

Theo pressed on, "The law clearly says that permits must be approved for posters and flyers dealing with politicians and people who are running for office, but not for anything else. These flyers are legal as long as they are taken down within ten days. That's the law."

"I don't like your attitude, kid," Bard shot back, puffing out his chest and actually putting a hand on his service revolver. Theo noticed the gun, but wasn't worried about being shot. Bard was trying to play the role of a tough cop, and he was not doing a very good job.

Being the only child of two lawyers, Theo had already developed a healthy suspicion of those people who thought they had more power than others, including policemen. He had been taught to respect all adults, especially those with authority, but at the same time, his parents had instilled in him a desire to always look for the truth. When a person—adult, teenager, child—was not being honest, then it was wrong to go along with their fraud or lie.

As everyone looked at Theo and waited on his response, he swallowed hard and said, "Well, sir, there's nothing wrong with my attitude. And, even if I had a bad attitude, it's not against the law."

Bard yanked a pen and a notepad from his pocket and said, "What's your name?"

Theo thought, I gave you my name three minutes ago, but he said, "Theodore Boone."

Bard scribbled this down in a flurry, as if whatever he was writing would one day carry great weight in a court of law. Everyone waited. Finally, one of the other officers took a few steps toward Bard and said, "Is your dad Woods Boone?" His nameplate identified him as Sneed.

*Finally,* Theo thought. "Yes, sir."

"And your mother's a lawyer, too, right?" Officer Sneed asked.

"Yes, sir."

Bard's shoulders slumped a few inches as he stopped scribbling on his pad. He looked puzzled, as if he was thinking, *Great. This kid knows the law and I don't, plus he's got two parents who'll probably sue me if I do something wrong.*

Sneed tried to help him by asking a pointless question. "You kids live around here?"

Darren slowly raised his hand and said, "I live a few blocks away, over on Emmitt Street."

The situation was sort of a standoff, with neither side sure what to do next. Sibley Taylor got off her bike and walked to a spot next to Theo. She smiled at Bard and Sneed, and said, "I don't understand. Why can't we work together here? April is our friend and we're very worried. The police are looking for her. We're looking for her. We're not doing anything wrong. What's the big deal?"

Bard and Sneed could think of no quick response to these simple questions with obvious answers.

In every class, there's always the kid who speaks before he thinks, or says what the others are thinking but are afraid to say. In this search party, that kid was Aaron Helleberg, who spoke English, German, and Spanish and got himself in trouble in all three. Aaron blurted, "Shouldn't you guys be looking for April instead of harassing us?"

Officer Bard sucked in his gut as if he'd been kicked there, and appeared ready to start shooting when Sneed jumped in. "Okay, here's the deal. You can hand out the flyers but you can't tack them onto city property—utility poles, bus-stop benches, things like that. It's almost five o'clock. I want you off the streets at six. Fair enough?" He was glaring at Theo when he finished.

Theo shrugged and said, "Fair enough." But it wasn't fair at all. They could tack the posters onto utility poles all day long. (But not city benches.) The police did not have the authority to change the city's laws, nor did they have the right to order the kids off the streets by 6:00 p.m.

However, at that moment a compromise was needed, and Sneed's deal was not that bad. The search would continue, and the police could say that they kept the kids in line. Solving a dispute often requires each side to back down a little, something else Theo had learned from his parents.

The search party biked back to Truman Park where it regrouped. Four of the kids had other things to do and left. Twenty minutes after they last saw Bard and Sneed, Theo and his gang moved into a neighborhood known as Maury Hill, in the southeast part of the city, as far away from Delmont as possible. They passed out dozens of flyers, inspected a few empty buildings, chatted with curious neighbors, and quit promptly at 6:00 p.m.

# Chapter 5

The Boone family dinner schedule was as predictable as a clock on the wall. On Mondays, they ate at Robilio's, an old Italian restaurant downtown, not far from the office. On Tuesdays, they ate soup and sandwiches at a homeless shelter where they volunteered. On Wednesdays, Mr. Boone picked up carryout Chinese from Dragon Lady, and they ate on folding trays as they watched television. On Thursdays, Mrs. Boone picked up a roasted chicken at a Turkish deli, and they ate it with hummus and pita bread. On Fridays, they ate fish at Malouf's, a popular restaurant owned by an old Lebanese couple who yelled at each other constantly. On Saturdays, each of the three

Boones took turns choosing what and where to eat. Theo usually preferred pizza and a movie. On Sundays, Mrs. Boone finally did her own cooking, which was Theo's least favorite meal of the week, though he was too smart to say so. Marcella didn't like to cook. She worked hard and spent long hours at the office, and simply did not enjoy rushing home and facing more work in the kitchen. Besides, there were plenty of good ethnic restaurants and delicatessens in Strattenburg, and it made much more sense to let real chefs do the cooking, at least in the opinion of Mrs. Marcella Boone. Theo didn't mind, nor did his father. When she did cook, she expected her husband and her son to clean up afterward, and both men preferred to avoid the dishwashing.

Dinner was always at 7:00 p.m. on the dot, another clear sign of organized people who hurried through each day with one eye on the clock. Theo placed his paper plate of chicken chow mein and sweet-and-sour shrimp on his TV tray and settled on the sofa. He then lowered a smaller plate onto the floor, where Judge was waiting with great anticipation. Judge loved Chinese food and expected to eat in the den with the humans. Dog food insulted him.

After a couple of bites, Mr. Boone asked, "So, Theo, any news on April?"

"No, sir. Just a lot of gossip at school."

"That poor child," Mrs. Boone said. "I'm sure everyone at school was worried."

"That's all we talked about. A total waste. I should stay home tomorrow and help with the search."

"That's a pretty lame effort," Mr. Boone said.

"Did you guys talk to the police about Mrs. Finnemore and explain to them that she's lying about being home with April? That she wasn't home Monday or Tuesday night? That she's a weirdo who's taking pills and neglecting her daughter?"

Silence. The room was quiet for a few seconds, then Mrs. Boone said, "No, Theo, we did not. We discussed it and decided to wait."

"But why?"

His father said, "Because it won't help the police find April. We plan to wait for a day or two. It's still being discussed."

"You're not eating, Theo," his mother said.

And it was true. He had no appetite. The food seemed to stop halfway down his esophagus, where a dull throbbing pain blocked everything. "I'm not hungry," he said.

Later, halfway through a rerun of *Law & Order*, a local newsbreak blasted out the latest. The search for April

Finnemore continued, with the police still tight-lipped about it. They flashed a photo of April, then one of the MISSING posters Theo and his gang had distributed. Immediately after this, there was the same ominous mug shot of Jack Leeper, looking like a serial killer. The reporter gushed, "The police are investigating the possibility that Jack Leeper, after his escape from prison in California, returned to Strattenburg to see his pen pal, April Finnemore."

The police are investigating a lot of things, Theo thought to himself. That doesn't mean they're all true. He had thought about Leeper all day, and he was certain that April would never open the door for such a creep. He had told himself over and over that the kidnapping theory could be nothing but one big coincidence: Leeper escaped from prison, returned to Strattenburg because he lived there many years ago, and got himself caught on videotape at a convenience store at the exact same time that April decided to run away.

Theo knew April well, but he also realized there were many things about her he didn't know. Nor did he want to. Was it possible that she would run away without a word to him? Slowly, he had begun to believe the answer was yes.

He was on the sofa under a quilt, with Judge wedged close to his chest, and at some point, both fell asleep. Theo had been awake since four thirty that morning and was sleep deprived. Physically and emotionally, he was exhausted.

# Chapter 6

The eastern boundary of the city of Strattenburg was formed by a bend in the Yancey River. An old bridge, one used by both cars and trains, crossed over into the next county. The bridge was not used much because there was little reason to travel into the next county. All of Strattenburg lay west of the river, and when leaving the city almost all traffic moved in that direction. In decades past, the Yancey had been a fairly important route for timber and crops, and in Strattenburg's early years the busy area "under the bridge" was notorious for saloons and illegal gambling halls and places for all sorts of bad behavior. When the river traffic declined, most of these places closed and the bad folks went elsewhere. However, enough stayed behind to ensure that the neighborhood would maintain its low reputation.

"Under the bridge" became simply "the bridge," a part of town that all decent people avoided. It was a dark place, almost hidden in the daytime by the shadows of a long bluff, with few streetlights at night and little traffic. There were bars and rough places where one went only to find trouble. The homes were small shacks built on stilts to protect them from high water. The people who lived there were sometimes called "river rats," a nickname they obviously found insulting. When they worked, they fished the Yancey and sold their catch to a cannery that produced cat and dog food. But they didn't work much. They were an idle people, living off the river, living off welfare, feuding with each other over trivial matters, and in general, earning their reputation as quick-tempered deadbeats.

Early Thursday morning, the manhunt arrived at the bridge.

A river rat named Buster Shell spent most of Wednesday evening in his favorite bar, drinking his favorite cheap beer and playing nickel-and-dime poker. When his money was gone, he had no choice but to leave and head home to his irritable wife and his three dirty children. As he walked through the narrow, unpaved streets, he bumped into a man who was going somewhere in a hurry. They exchanged a couple of harsh words, as was the custom under the bridge, but the other man showed no interest in a fistfight, something Buster was certainly ready for.

As Buster resumed his walk, he stopped dead cold. He'd seen that face before. He'd seen it only hours earlier. It was the face of that guy the cops were searching for. What's his name? Buster, half drunk or worse, snapped his fingers in the middle of the street as he racked his brain trying to remember.

"Leeper," he finally said. "Jack Leeper."

By now, most of Strattenburg knew that a reward of five thousand dollars was being offered by the police for any information leading to the arrest of Jack Leeper. Buster could almost smell the money. He looked around, but the man was long gone. However, Leeper—and there was no doubt in Buster's mind that the man was indeed Jack Leeper—was now somewhere under the bridge. He was in Buster's part of town, a place the police preferred to avoid, a place where the river rats made their own rules.

Within minutes, Buster had rounded up a small, well-armed posse, half a dozen men about as drunk as he was. Word was out. The rumor that the escaped convict was in the vicinity roared through the neighborhood. The river people fought constantly among themselves, but when threatened from the outside, they quickly circled the wagons.

With Buster giving orders that no one followed, the search for Leeper sputtered from the start. There was considerable conflict in terms of strategy, and since every man carried a loaded gun, the disagreements were serious. With time, though, they agreed that the one main street that led up the bluff and into town should be guarded. When that was done, Leeper's only chance of escape was either by stealing a boat or going for a swim in the Yancey River.

Hours passed. Buster and his men went door-to-door, carefully searching under the houses, behind the shanties, inside the small stores and shops, through the thickets and underbrush. The search party grew and grew and Buster began to worry about how they might split the reward money with so many people now involved. How could he keep most of the money? It would be difficult. The payment of five thousand dollars to a bunch of river rats would ignite a small war under the bridge.

The first hint of sunlight peeked through the clouds far to the east. The search was running out of gas. Buster's recruits were tired and losing their enthusiasm.

Miss Ethel Barber was eighty-five years old and had lived alone since her husband died years earlier. She was one of the few residents under the bridge who was missing the excitement. When she awoke at 6:00 a.m. and went to make coffee, she heard a faint noise coming from the rear door of her four-room shanty. She kept a pistol in a drawer under the toaster. She grabbed it, then flipped on a light switch. Like Buster, she came face-to-face with the man she'd seen on the local news. He was in the process of removing a screen from the small window on the door, obviously trying to break in. When Miss Ethel raised her gun, as if to shoot through the window, Jack Leeper's jaw dropped, his eyes widened in horror, and he uttered some gasp of shock that she couldn't quite make out. (She had lost most of her hearing anyway.) Leeper then ducked quickly and scrambled away. Miss Ethel grabbed her phone and called 911.

Within ten minutes, a police helicopter was hovering near the bridge and the SWAT team was moving silently through the streets.

Buster Shell was arrested for public drunkenness, unlawful possession of a firearm, and resisting arrest. He was handcuffed and taken to the city jail, his dreams of reward money dashed forever.

———————

They soon found Leeper, in an overgrown ditch near the street that led to and from the bridge. He had circled back and was evidently trying to leave the area. Why he went there in the first place would remain a mystery.

He was spotted by the helicopter crew. The SWAT team was directed to his hiding place, and within minutes the street was filled with police cars, armed officers of all varieties, sharpshooters, bloodhounds, even an ambulance. The helicopter got lower and lower. No one wanted to miss the fun. There was a van from the television news channel, filming live coverage.

Theo was watching. He was up early because he'd been up most of the night, tossing and flipping in his bed, worrying about April. He sat at the kitchen table, toying with a bowl of cereal, watching the small screen on the counter with his parents. When the camera offered a close-up of the SWAT team dragging someone from the ditch, Theo dropped his spoon, picked up the remote, and increased the volume.

The sight of Jack Leeper was frightening. His clothes were torn and covered with mud. He had not shaved in days. His thick black hair was wild and shooting in all directions. He appeared angry and defiant, yapping at the police and even spitting at the camera. As he neared the street and was surrounded by even more officers, a reporter yelled, "Hey, Leeper! Where's April Finnemore!?"

To which Leeper offered a nasty grin and yelled back, "You'll never find her."

"Is she alive?"

"You'll never find her."

"Oh, my God," Mrs. Boone said.

Theo's heart froze and he couldn't breathe. He watched as Leeper was shoved into the rear of a police van and driven away. The reporter was talking to the camera, but Theo didn't hear his words. He gently placed his head in his hands, and began to cry.

# Chapter 7

First period was Spanish, Theo's second favorite class, just behind Government with Mr. Mount. Spanish was taught by Madame Monique, a young, pretty, exotic lady from Cameroon, in West Africa. Spanish was just one of many languages she spoke. Normally, the sixteen boys in Theo's section were easy to motivate and enjoyed the class.

Today, though, the entire school was in a daze. Yesterday, the halls and classrooms were filled with nervous chatter as the rumors spread about April's disappearance. Was she kidnapped? Did she run away? What's up with her weird mother? Where's her father? These questions and more were tossed up for debate and kicked around with great enthusiasm throughout the day. Now, though, with the capture of Jack Leeper, and the unforgettable words he uttered about April, the students and teachers were in a state of fear and disbelief.

Madame Monique understood the situation. She taught April, too, in a girl's section during fourth period. She tried to engage the boys in a halfhearted discussion about Mexican food, but they were too distracted.

During second period, the entire eighth grade was called into an assembly in the auditorium. Five sections of girls, five of boys, along with all the teachers. The middle school was in its third year of an experiment which separated the genders during classroom instruction, but not during the rest of the day's activities. So far, the experiment was getting favorable reviews. But, because they were separated for most of the day, when they came together at lunch, morning break, physical education, or assembly, there was a bit more electricity in the air and it took a few minutes to calm things. Not today, though. They were subdued. There was none of the usual posturing, flirting, gazing, or nervous chatter. They took their seats quietly, somberly.

The principal, Mrs. Gladwell, spent some time trying to convince them that April was probably all right, that the police were confident she would be found soon and returned to school. Her voice was comforting, her words were reassuring, and the eighth graders were ready to believe any good news. Then a noise—the unmistakable thumping of a low-flying helicopter—passed over the school, and all thoughts immediately returned to the frantic search for their classmate. A few of the girls could be seen rubbing their eyes.

Later, after lunch, as Theo and his friends were in the middle of a halfhearted game of Frisbee football, another helicopter buzzed over the school, obviously going somewhere in a hurry. From its markings, it appeared to be from some branch of law enforcement. The game stopped; the boys stared upward until the chopper was gone. The bell rang, ending lunch, and the boys quietly returned to class.

Throughout the school day, there were times when Theo and his friends were almost able to forget about April, if only for a moment. And whenever these moments occurred, and they were indeed rare, another helicopter could be heard somewhere over Strattenburg—buzzing, thumping, watching—like some giant insect ready to attack.

The entire city was on edge, as if waiting for horrible news. In the cafés and shops and offices downtown, the employees and customers chatted in hushed tones and repeated whatever rumors they'd heard in the past thirty minutes. In the courthouse, always a rich source of gossip, the clerks and lawyers huddled around coffeepots and watercoolers and exchanged the latest. The local television stations offered live reports on the half hour. These breathless updates usually offered nothing new, just a reporter somewhere near the river saying pretty much what he or she had said earlier.

At Strattenburg Middle School, the eighth graders quietly went through their daily schedules, most of them anxious to get home.

Jack Leeper, now wearing an orange jumpsuit with CITY JAIL stenciled in black letters across the front and back, was led to an interrogation room in the basement of the Strattenburg Police Department. In the center of the room, there was a small table, and a folding chair for the suspect. Across the table sat two detectives, Slater and Capshaw. The uniformed officers escorting Leeper removed the handcuffs and ankle chains, then retreated to their positions by the door. They remained in the room for protection, though they were not really needed. Detectives Slater and Capshaw could certainly take care of themselves.

"Have a seat, Mr. Leeper," Detective Slater said, waving at the empty folding chair. Leeper slowly sat down. He had showered but not shaved, and still looked like some deranged cult leader who'd just spent a month or so in the woods.

"I'm Detective Slater, and this is my partner Detective Capshaw."

"A real pleasure to meet you boys," Leeper said with a snarl.

"Oh, the pleasure is ours," Slater said, with equal sarcasm.

"A real honor," Capshaw said, one of the few times he would speak.

Slater was a veteran detective, the highest ranking, and the best in Strattenburg. He was wiry with a slick, shaved head, and he wore nothing but black suits with black ties. The city saw very little in the way of violent crime, but when they did Detective Slater was there to solve it and bring the felon to justice. His sidekick, Capshaw, was the observer, the note taker, the nicer of the two when they found it necessary to play good cop/bad cop.

"We'd like to ask you some questions," Slater said. "You wanna talk?"

"Maybe."

Capshaw whipped out a sheet of paper and handed it to Slater, who said, "Well, Mr. Leeper, as you well know from your long career as a professional thug, you must first be advised of your rights. You do remember this, don't you?"

Leeper glared at Slater as if he might reach across the table and grab his throat, but Slater was not the least bit worried.

"You've heard of the *Miranda* rights, haven't you, Mr. Leeper?" Slater continued.

"Yep."

"Of course you have. I'm sure you've been in many of these rooms over the years," Slater said with a nasty grin. Leeper was not grinning. Capshaw was already taking notes.

Slater continued: "First of all, you're not required to talk to us. Period. Understand?"

Leeper shook his head, yes.

"But if you do talk to us, then anything you say can be used against you in court. Got it?"

"Yep."

"You have the right to a lawyer, to legal advice. Understand?"

"Yep."

"And if you can't afford one, which I'm sure you cannot, then the State will provide one for you. Are you with me?"

"Yep."

Slater slid the sheet of paper close to Leeper and said, "If you sign here, then you agree that I've explained your rights and that you are voluntarily waiving them." He placed a pen on top of the paper. Leeper took his time, read the words, fiddled with the pen, then finally signed his name. "Can I have some coffee?" he asked.

"Cream and sugar?" Slater asked.

"No, just black."

Slater nodded at one of the uniformed officers, who left the room.

"Now, we have some questions for you," Slater said. "Are you ready to talk?"

"Maybe."

"Two weeks ago, you were in prison in California, serving a life sentence for kidnapping. You escaped through a tunnel with six others, and now you're here in Strattenburg."

"You got a question?"

"Yes, Mr. Leeper, I have a question. Why did you come to Strattenburg?"

"I had to go somewhere. Couldn't just hang around outside the prison, know what I mean?"

"I suppose. You lived here once, correct?"

"When I was a kid, sixth grade, I think. Went to the middle school for a year, then we moved off."

"And you have relatives in the area?"

"Some distant kin."

"One of those distant relatives is Imelda May Underwood, whose mother had a third cousin named Ruby Dell Butts, whose father was Franklin Butts, better known out in Massey's Mill as 'Logchain' Butts, and 'Logchain' had a half-brother named Winstead Leeper, 'Winky' for short, and I believe he was your father. Died about ten years ago."

Leeper absorbed all this and finally said, "Winky Leeper was my father, yes."

"So somewhere in the midst of all this divorcing and remarrying, you came to be a tenth or eleventh cousin of Imelda May Underwood, who married a man named Thomas Finnemore and now goes by the name of May Finnemore, mother of young April. This sound right to you, Mr. Leeper?"

"I never had any use for my family."

"Well, I'm sure they're real proud of you, too."

The door opened and the officer placed a paper cup of steaming black coffee on the table in front of Leeper. It appeared to be too hot to drink, so Leeper just stared at it. Slater paused for a second, then pressed on. "We have copies of five letters April wrote to you in prison. Sweet, kid stuff—she felt sorry for you and wanted to be pen pals. Did you write her back?"

"Yep."

"How often?"

"I don't know. Several times, I guess."

"Did you come back to Strattenburg to see April?"

Leeper finally picked up the cup and took a sip of coffee. Slowly, he said, "I'm not sure I want to answer that question."

For the first time, Detective Slater seemed to become irritated. "Why are you afraid of that question, Mr. Leeper?"

"I don't have to answer your question. Says so right there on your little piece of paper. I can walk out right now. I know the rules."

"Did you come here to see April?"

Leeper took another sip, and for a long time nothing was said. The four officers stared at him. He stared at the paper cup. Finally, he said, "Look, here's the situation. You want something. I want something. You want the girl. I want a deal."

"What kind of a deal, Leeper?" Slater shot back.

"Just a moment ago it was Mr. Leeper. Now, just Leeper. Do I frustrate you, Detective? If so, I'm real sorry. Here's what I have in mind. I know I'm going back to prison, but I'm really tired of California. The prisons are brutal— overcrowded, lots of gangs, violence, rotten food—you know what I mean, Detective Slater?"

Slater had never been inside a prison, but to move things along he said, "Sure."

"I want to do my time here, where the slammers are a bit nicer. I know because I've had a good look at them."

"Where's the girl, Leeper?" Slater said. "If you kidnapped her, you're looking at another life sentence. If she's dead, you're looking at capital murder and death row."

"Why would I harm my little cousin?"

"Where is she, Leeper?"

Another long sip of coffee, then Leeper crossed his arms over his chest and grinned at Detective Slater. Seconds ticked away.

"You're playing games, Leeper," Detective Capshaw said.

"Maybe, maybe not. Is there any reward money on the table?"

"Not for you," Slater said.

"Why not? You give me some money, I'll take you to the girl."

"It doesn't work that way."

"Fifty thousand bucks, and you can have her."

"What will you do with fifty thousand bucks, Leeper?" Slater asked. "You're in prison for the rest of your life."

"Oh, money goes a long way in prison. You get me the

money, and you arrange things so I can serve my time here, and we got a deal."

"You're dumber than I thought," Slater said, frustrated.

Capshaw added quickly, "And we thought you were pretty dumb before we got started with this conversation."

"Come on, boys. That gets you nowhere. We got a deal?"

"No deal, Leeper," Slater said.

"That's too bad."

"No deal, but I'll make a promise. If that girl is harmed in any way, I'll hound you to your grave."

Leeper laughed loudly, then said, "I love it when the cops start making threats. It's over, boys. I ain't talking no more."

"Where's the girl, Leeper?" Capshaw asked.

Leeper just grinned and shook his head.

# Chapter 8

Theo preferred not to stay at school after classes and watch the girls play soccer. He himself did not play soccer, not that he had the choice. An asthma condition kept him away from strenuous activities, but even without the asthma he doubted he would be playing soccer. He had tried it as a six-year-old, before the asthma, and never got the hang of it. When he was nine, while playing baseball, he collapsed at third base after hitting a triple, and that ended his short career in team sports. He took up golf.

Mr. Mount, though, loved soccer, had even played in college, and was offering extra credit to students who hung around for the game. Plus, there was an unwritten rule at Strattenburg Middle School that the girls cheered for the boys, and vice versa. Any other time, Theo would have happily watched from the bleachers, taking casual notice of the game but really sizing up the twenty-two girls on the field and those on the bench as well. But not today. He wanted to be elsewhere, on his bike, handing out the MISSING flyers, doing something to aid in the search for April.

It was a terrible day for a game of any kind. The Strattenburg kids were distracted. The players and their fans lacked energy. Even the opposing team, from Elksburg, forty miles away, seemed subdued. When another helicopter flew over ten minutes into the game, every girl on the field paused for a second and looked up in apprehension.

As expected, Mr. Mount gradually made his way over to a group of women. The worst kept secret at school was that Mr. Mount had his eye on Miss Highlander, a stunning seventh-grade math teacher just two years out of college. Every boy in the seventh and eighth grades had a desperate, secret crush on Miss Highlander, and evidently Mr. Mount had some interest as well. He was in his mid-thirties, single, by far the coolest male teacher in the school, and the sixteen boys in his homeroom were aggressively pushing him to pursue Miss Highlander.

When Mr. Mount began to make his move, so did Theo. He assumed correctly that Mr. Mount's attention would soon be focused elsewhere; it was the perfect time for a quiet exit. Theo and three others drifted from the soccer field and were soon on their bikes racing away from the school. Their search party was much smaller, and this was by design. Yesterday's had too many kids, with too many opinions, and too much activity that might be noticed by cops such as Officer Bard. Plus, there had been fewer volunteers during the school day as Theo and Woody got things organized. The sense of urgency that Theo felt was not shared by many of his classmates. They were concerned all right, but many of them thought that searches by kids on bikes were a waste of time. The police had SWAT teams, helicopters, dogs, and no shortage of manpower. If they couldn't find April, the search was hopeless.

Theo, along with Woody, Aaron, and Chase, returned to the Delmont neighborhood and roamed the streets for a few minutes to make sure the police were elsewhere. With no cops in sight, they quickly began passing out MISSING flyers and tacking them to utility poles. They inspected a few empty buildings, looked behind some run-down apartments, picked their way through an overgrown drainage ditch, checked under two bridges, and were making real progress when Woody's older brother called his cell phone. Woody froze, listened intently, then reported to the gang, "They've found something down by the river."

"What?"

"Not sure, but my brother is monitoring his police scanner, said the thing has gone crazy with chatter. All cops are headed down there."

Without hesitation, Theo said, "Let's go."

They sped away, out of Delmont, past Stratten College, into downtown, and as they approached the east end of Main Street, they saw police cars and dozens of officers milling about. The street was blocked; the area under the bridge was sealed off. The air was heavy with tension. And noise—two helicopters were hovering over the river. The downtown merchants and their customers stood on the sidewalks, gawking into the distance, waiting for something to happen. Traffic was being diverted away from the bridge and the river.

As the boys watched, another police car crept up beside them. The driver rolled down his window, then snarled, "What are you boys doing here?" It was Officer Bard, again.

"We're just riding our bikes," Theo said. "It's not against the law."

"Don't get smart with me, Boone. If I see you boys anywhere near the river, I swear I'll take you in."

Theo thought of several quick retorts, all of which

would lead to more trouble. So he gritted his teeth and politely said, "Yes, sir."

Bard smiled smugly, then drove away, toward the bridge.

"Follow me," Woody said as they raced off. Woody lived in a section of town called East Bluff, near the river, on a gentle rise that eventually gave way to the lowlands around the water. It was a notorious place, full of narrow streets, dark alleys, creeks, and dead-end roads. The neighborhood was generally safe, but it produced more than its share of colorful stories of strange events. Woody's father was a noted stonemason who'd lived his entire life in East Bluff. It was a large clannish family, with lots of aunts, uncles, and cousins, all living close to each other.

Ten minutes after their encounter with Officer Bard, the boys were zipping through East Bluff, along a narrow dirt trail that zigzagged high above and beside the river. Woody was pedaling like a madman and making it difficult for the others to keep up. This was his turf; he'd been riding his bike through these trails since he was six. They crossed a gravel road, plunged down a steep hill, shot up the other side, and got serious air before landing back on the trail. Theo, Aaron, and Chase were terrified but too excited to slow down. And, of course, they were determined to keep up with Woody, who was prone to talk trash at any moment. They finally slid to a stop at a small overlook, a grassy area where the river could be seen below through some trees. "Follow me," Woody said, and they left their bikes behind. Clutching a vine, they scampered down the side of a cliff to a rocky landing, and there, below, was the Yancey River. Their view was unobstructed.

A mile or two away, to the north, were the rows of small whitewashed houses where the river rats lived, and beyond them was the bridge, crawling with police cars. On the other side of the river, close to the bridge, an ambulance was just arriving on the scene. Policemen were in boats; several were in full scuba gear. The situation looked tense, almost frantic, as sirens wailed, policemen darted about, and the helicopters hovered low, watching everything.

Something had been found.

The boys sat on the cliff for a long time and said little. The search, or rescue, or removal, or whatever it was called, was proceeding slowly. Each of them had the same thought— that they were watching an actual crime scene in which the victim was their friend April Finnemore, and that she'd been harmed in some terrible way and left at the edge of the river. She was apparently dead, since there was no urgency in getting her out of the water and to a hospital. More police cars arrived, more chaos.

Finally, Chase said, to no one in particular, "Do you think it's April?"

To which Woody abruptly responded, "Who else would it be? It's not every day that a dead body floats into town."

"You don't know who it is or what it is," Aaron said. He usually found some way to disagree with Woody, who had quick opinions about almost everything.

Theo's cell phone buzzed in his pocket. He glanced at it—Mrs. Boone on her office line. "It's my mom," he said nervously, then answered his phone.

"Hi, Mom."

On the other end, his mother said, "Theo, where are you?"

"Just left the soccer game," he said, wincing at his friends. It wasn't a complete fib, but it was also pretty far from the truth.

"Well, it appears as though the police have found a body in the river, on the other side, near the bridge," she said. One of the helicopters, red and yellow with Channel 5 painted boldly on the sides, was obviously sending a live feed back to the station, and the entire town was probably watching.

"Has it been identified?" Theo asked.

"No, not yet. But it can't be good news, Theo."

"This is awful."

"When are you coming to the office?"

"I'll be there in twenty minutes."

"Okay, Theo. Please be careful."

The ambulance was moving away from the river, then onto the bridge, where a line of police cars formed an escort. The procession picked up speed over the river, with the helicopters trailing behind.

"Let's go," Theo said, and the boys slowly climbed up the cliff and left on their bikes.

Boone & Boone had a large law library on its first floor, near the front, close to where Elsa worked, keeping an eye on everything. The library was Theo's favorite room in the building. He loved its rows of thick, important books, its large leather chairs, and its long mahogany conference table. It was used for all sorts of big meetings—depositions, settlement talks, and, for Mrs. Boone, pretrial preparation. She occasionally went to trial in divorce cases. Mr. Boone did not. He was a real estate lawyer who seldom left his upstairs office. He did, though, need the library from time to time to close real estate deals.

They were waiting for Theo in the library. A large flat-screen television was on with the local news, and his parents and Elsa were watching. His mother hugged him when he walked in, then Elsa hugged him, too. He took a seat near the television, his mother on one side, Elsa on the other, both patting his knees as if he had just been rescued from near death. The news report was all about the discovery of a body and its transport to the city morgue where authorities were now doing all sorts of important stuff. The reporter wasn't sure what was happening in the morgue, and she was unable to find a witness willing to talk, so she just prattled on the way they normally do.

Theo wanted to tell everyone that he'd had a bird's-eye view down at the river, but such a statement would make things complicated.

The reporter said the police were working with inspectors from the state crime lab and hoped to know more within a few hours.

"That poor girl," Elsa said, and not for the first time.

"Why do you say that?" Theo asked.

"I beg your pardon."

"You don't know it's a girl. You don't know it's April. We don't know anything, right?"

The adults glanced at each other. Both women continued patting Theo's knees.

"Theo's right," Mr. Boone said, but only to comfort his son.

They flashed a picture of Jack Leeper for the one hundredth time, and gave his background. When it became apparent there was nothing new at the moment, the story grew old. Mr. Boone drifted away. Mrs. Boone had a client waiting in the lobby. Elsa needed to answer the phone.

Theo eventually made his way to his office at the rear of the building. Judge followed, and Theo spent a lot of time rubbing his dog's head and talking to him. It made both of them feel better. Theo put his feet on his desk and looked around his small office. He focused on the wall where his favorite sketch always made him smile. It was an elaborate pencil drawing of young Theodore Boone, Attorney, in court wearing a suit and tie, with a gavel flying by his head and the jurors roaring with laughter. The caption screamed, "Overruled!" At the bottom right-hand corner, the artist had scribbled her name, *April Finnemore*. The drawing had been a gift for Theo's birthday the year before.

Was her career over before it started? Was April dead, a sweet thirteen-year-old kid brutally abducted and killed because there was no one to take care of her? Theo's hands were shaking and his mouth was dry. He closed and locked his door, then walked to the drawing and gently touched her name. His eyes were moist, then he began crying. He dropped to the floor and cried for a long time. Judge settled in next to him, watching him sadly.

# Chapter 9

An hour passed and darkness settled in. Theo sat at his small desk, a card table equipped with lawyerly things—a daily planner, a small digital clock, a fake fountain pen set, his own nameplate carved in wood. Before him was an open Algebra textbook. He'd been staring at it for a long time, unable to read the words or turn the pages. His notebook was open, too, and the page was blank.

He could think of nothing but April, and the horror of watching from a distance as the police fished her body from the backwaters of the Yancey River. He had not actually seen a body, but he'd seen the police and scuba divers surround something and work frantically to remove it. Obviously, it was a body. A dead person. Why else would the police be there, doing what they were doing? There had been no other missing persons in Strattenburg in the past week, or the past year, for that matter. The list had only one name on it, and Theo was convinced that April was dead. Abducted and murdered and thrown in the water by Jack Leeper.

Theo couldn't wait for Leeper's trial. He hoped it would happen soon, just a few blocks away in the county courthouse. He would watch every moment of it, even if he had to skip school. Maybe he would be called as a witness. He wasn't sure what he would say on the witness stand, but he would say whatever it took to nail Leeper, to get him convicted and sent away forever. It would be a great moment—Theo being called as a witness, walking into the packed courtroom, placing his hand on the Bible, swearing to tell the truth, taking his seat in the witness box, smiling up at Judge Henry Gantry, glancing confidently at the curious faces of the jurors, taking in the large audience, then glaring at the hideous face of Jack Leeper, staring him down in open court, fearless. The more Theo thought about this scene, the more he liked it. There was a good chance Theo was the last person to talk to April before she was abducted. He could testify that she was frightened, and, surprisingly, alone. Entry! That would be the issue. How did the attacker get into the house? Perhaps only Theo knew that she had locked all the doors and windows and even jammed chairs under doorknobs because she was so frightened. So, since there were no signs of a break-in, she knew the identity of her abductor. She knew Jack Leeper. Somehow he'd been able to persuade her to open the door.

As Theo replayed his last conversation with April, he became convinced that he would indeed be called by the prosecution as a witness. For a few moments, he visualized himself in the courtroom, then he suddenly forgot about it. The shock of the tragedy returned, and he realized his eyes were moist again. His throat was tight and his stomach ached, and Theo needed to be around another human. Elsa was gone for the day, as were Dorothy and Vince. His mother had a client in her office with the door locked. His father was upstairs pushing paper around his desk and trying to finish some big deal. Theo stood, stepped over Judge, and looked at the sketch April had given him. Again, he touched her name.

They met in prekindergarten, though Theo couldn't remember exactly when or how. Four-year-olds don't actually meet and introduce themselves. They just sort of show up at school and get to know each other. April was in his class. Mrs. Sansing was the teacher. In the first and second grades, April was in another section, and Theo hardly saw her. By the third grade, the natural forces of aging had kicked in and the boys wanted nothing to do with the girls, and vice versa. Theo vaguely recalled that April moved away for a year or two. He forgot about her, as did most of the kids in his grade. But he remembered the day she returned. He was sitting in Mr. Hancock's sixth-grade class during the second week of school when the door opened and April walked in. She was escorted by an assistant principal who introduced her and explained that her family had just moved back to Strattenburg. She seemed embarrassed by the attention, and when she sat at a desk next to Theo, she glanced at him and smiled and said, "Hi, Theo." He smiled but was unable to respond.

Most of the class remembered her, and though she was quiet, almost shy, she had no trouble resuming old friendships with the girls. She wasn't popular because she didn't try to be. She wasn't unpopular because she was genuinely nice and thoughtful and acted more mature than most of her classmates. She was odd enough to keep the others guessing. She dressed more like a boy and wore her hair very short. She didn't like sports or television or the Internet. Instead, she painted and studied art and talked of living in Paris or Santa Fe where she would do nothing but paint. She loved contemporary art that baffled her classmates and teachers alike.

Soon there were rumors about her weird family, of siblings named after the months, of a wacky mother who peddled goat cheese, and of an absentee father. Throughout the sixth grade and into the seventh, April became more withdrawn and moodier. She said very little in class and missed more school days than any other student.

As the hormones kicked in and the gender walls came down, it slowly became cool for a boy to have a girlfriend. The cuter and more popular girls were chased and caught, but not April. She showed no interest in boys and didn't have a clue when it came to flirting. She was aloof, often lost in her own world. Theo liked her; he had for a long time, but was too shy and too self-conscious to make a move. He wasn't sure how to make a move, and April seemed unapproachable.

It happened in gym class, on a cold snowy afternoon in late February. Two sections of seventh graders had just begun a one-hour torture session under the command of Mr. Bart Tyler, a young hotshot physical education teacher who fancied himself as a Marine drill instructor. The students, both boys and girls, had just completed a set of brutal wind sprints when Theo suddenly could not catch his breath. He ran for his backpack in a corner, pulled out his inhaler, and took several puffs of medication. This happened occasionally, and, though his classmates understood, Theo was always embarrassed. He was actually exempt from gym, but he insisted on participating.

Mr. Tyler showed the right amount of concern and led Theo to a spot in the bleachers. He was humiliated. As Mr. Tyler walked away and began blowing his whistle and yelling, April Finnemore left the crowd and took a seat next to Theo. Very close.

"Are you all right?" she asked.

"I'm fine," he answered as he began to think that maybe an asthma attack wasn't so bad after all. She placed a hand on his knee and looked at him with tremendous concern.

A loud voice yelled, "Hey, April, what are you doing?" It was Mr. Tyler.

She coolly turned and said, "I'm taking a break."

"Oh really. I don't recall approving a break. Get back in line."

To which she repeated, icily, "I said I'm taking a break."

Mr. Tyler paused for a second, then managed to say, "And why is that?"

"Because I have an asthma condition, just like Theo."

At that point, no one knew if April was telling the truth, but no one, especially Mr. Tyler, seemed willing to push harder. "All right, all right," he said, and then blew his whistle at the rest of the kids. For the first time in his young life, Theo was thrilled to have asthma.

For the remainder of the period, Theo and April sat knee-to-knee in the bleachers, watching the others sweat and groan, giggling at the less-than-athletic ones, mocking Mr. Tyler, gossiping about the classmates they were not so fond of, and whispering about life in general. That night, they Facebooked for the first time.

A sudden knock on the door startled Theo, followed by his father's voice. "Theo, open up."

Theo quickly stepped to the door, unlocked and opened it. "Are you okay?" Mr. Boone asked.

"Sure, Dad."

"Look, there are a couple of policemen here and they would like to talk to you."

Theo was too confused to respond. His father continued, "I'm not sure what they want, probably just more background on April. Let's talk to them in the library. Both your mother and I will be with you."

"Uh, okay."

They met in the library. Detectives Slater and Capshaw were standing and chatting gravely with Mrs. Boone when Theo walked in. Introductions were made, seats were taken.

Theo was secured with a parent/lawyer on each side. The detectives were directly across the table. As usual, Slater did the talking and Capshaw took the notes.

Slater began, "Sorry to barge in like this, but you may have heard that a body was pulled from the river this afternoon."

All three Boones nodded. Theo was not about to admit that he'd watched the police from a cliff across the river. He was not about to say any more than necessary.

Slater went on, "The crime lab people are at work right now trying to identify the body. Frankly, it is not easy because the body is well, shall we say, somewhat decomposed."

The knot in Theo's chest grew tighter. His throat ached and he told himself not to start crying. April, decomposed? He just wanted to go home, go to his room, lock his door, lie on his bed, stare at the ceiling, then go into a coma and wake up in a year.

"We've talked to her mother," Slater said softly, with great patience and compassion, "and she tells us that you were April's best friend. You guys talked all the time, hung out a lot. That true?"

Theo shook his head but could not speak.

Slater glanced at Capshaw who returned the glance without stopping his pen.

"What we need, Theo, is any information about what

April might have been wearing when she disappeared," Slater said. Capshaw added, "The body at the crime lab has the remains of some clothing on it. It could help with identification."

As soon as Capshaw paused, Slater moved in, "We've made an inventory of her clothing, with her mother's help. She said that perhaps you'd given her an item or two. A baseball jacket of some sort."

Theo swallowed hard and tried to speak clearly. "Yes, sir. Last year I gave April a Twins baseball jacket and a Twins cap."

Capshaw wrote even faster. Slater said, "Can you describe this jacket?"

Theo shrugged and said, "Sure. It was dark blue with red trim, Minnesota colors, with the word TWINS across the back in red-and-white lettering."

"Leather, cloth, cotton, synthetic?"

"I don't know, synthetic maybe. I think the lining on the inside was cotton, but I'm not sure."

The two detectives exchanged ominous looks.

"Can I ask why you gave it to her?" Slater said.

"Sure. I won it in an online contest at the Twins website, and since I already had two or three Twins jackets, I gave it to April. It was a medium, kid's size, too small for me."

"She a baseball fan?" Capshaw asked.

"Not really. She doesn't like sports. The gift was sort of a joke."

"Did she wear it often?"

"I never saw her wear it. I don't think she wore the cap either."

"Why the Twins?" Capshaw asked.

"Is that really important?" Mrs. Boone shot across the table. Capshaw flinched as though he'd been slapped.

"No, sorry."

"Where is this going?" Mr. Boone demanded.

Both detectives exhaled in unison, then took another breath. Slater said, "We have not found such a jacket in April's closet or anywhere in her room, or the house for that matter. I guess we can assume she was wearing it when she left. The temperature was around sixty degrees, so she probably grabbed the nearest jacket."

"And the clothing on the body?" Mrs. Boone asked.

Both detectives squirmed in unison, then glanced at each other. Slater said, "We really can't say at this time, Mrs. Boone." They may have been prohibited from saying anything, but their body language was not difficult to read. The jacket Theo had just described matched whatever they'd found on the body. At least in Theo's opinion.

His parents nodded as if they understood completely,

but Theo did not. He had a dozen questions for the police, but didn't have the energy to start firing away.

"What about dental records?" Mr. Boone asked.

Both detectives frowned and shook their heads. "Not possible," Slater said. The answer provoked all manner of horrible images. The body was so mangled and damaged that the jaws were missing.

Mrs. Boone jumped in quickly with, "What about DNA testing?"

"In the works," Slater said, "but it'll take at least three days."

Capshaw slowly closed his notepad and put his pen in a pocket. Slater glanced at his watch. The detectives were suddenly ready to leave. They had the information they were after, and if they stayed longer there might be more questions about the investigation from the Boone family, questions they did not want to answer.

They thanked Theo, expressed their concerns about his friend, and said good night to Mr. and Mrs. Boone.

Theo stayed in his seat at the table, staring blankly at the wall, his thoughts a jumbled mess of fear, sadness, and disbelief.

# Chapter 10

Chase Whipple's mother was also a lawyer. His father sold computers and had installed the system at the Boone law firm. The families were good friends, and at some point during the afternoon, the mothers decided that the boys needed some diversion. Perhaps everyone needed something else to think about.

For as long as Theo could remember, his parents had held season tickets for all home basketball and football games at Stratten College, a small, liberal arts, Division III school, eight blocks from downtown. They bought the tickets for several reasons: one, to support the local team; two, to actually watch a few games, though Mrs. Boone disliked football and could pass on basketball; and, three, to satisfy the college's athletic director, a feisty man known to call fans himself and badger them into supporting the teams. Such was life in a small town. If the Boones couldn't make a game, the tickets were usually given to clients. It was good business.

The Boones met the Whipples at the ticket window outside Memorial Hall, a 1920s-style gymnasium in the center of the campus. They hurried inside and found their seats—mid-court and ten rows up. The game was three minutes old and the Stratten student section had already reached full volume. Theo sat next to Chase, at the end of the row. Both mothers kept looking at the boys, as if they needed some type of special observation on this awful day.

Chase, like Theo, enjoyed sports, but was more of a spectator than an athlete. Chase was a mad scientist, a genius in certain fields; a violent experimental chemist who'd burned down the family's storage shed with one project and nearly vaporized the family's garage with another. His experiments were legendary and every science teacher at Strattenburg Middle School kept a close eye on him. When Chase was in the lab, nothing was safe. He was also a computer whiz, a techno-geek, a superb hacker, which had also caused some problems.

"What's the line?" Theo whispered to Chase.

"Stratten's favored by eight."

"Says who?"

"Greensheet." Division III basketball games were not favored by gamblers and oddsmakers, but there were a few offshore websites where one could find a line and place a bet. Theo and Chase did not gamble, nor did anyone they knew, but it was always interesting to know which team was favored.

"I hear you guys were down at the river when they found the body," Chase said, careful not to be heard by anyone around them.

"Who told you?"

"Woody. He told me everything."

"We didn't see a body, okay. We saw something, but it was pretty far away."

"I guess it had to be the body, right? I mean, the police found a body in the river, and you guys watched it all."

"Let's talk about something else, Chase. Okay?"

Chase had shown little interest in girls so far, and even less interest in April. And she had certainly shown no interest in him. Other than Theo, April didn't care for boys.

There was a time-out on the court, and the Stratten cheerleaders came tumbling out of the stands, hopping and bouncing and flinging each other through the air. Theo and Chase grew still and watched closely. For two thirteen-year-olds, the brief performances by the cheerleaders were captivating.

When the time-out ended, the teams took the court and the game resumed. Mrs. Boone turned and looked down at the boys. Then Mrs. Whipple did the same.

"Why do they keep looking at us?" Theo mumbled to Chase.

"Because they're worried about us. That's why we're here, Theo. That's why we're going out for pizza after the game. They think we're real fragile right now because some thug who escaped from prison snatched one of our classmates and threw her in the river. My mom said that all parents are sort of protective right now."

The Stratten point guard, who was well under six feet tall, slam-dunked the ball and the crowd went wild. Theo tried to forget about April, and Chase as well, and concentrated on the game. At halftime, the boys went to get popcorn. Theo made a quick call to Woody for an update. Woody and his brother were monitoring a police radio and surfing online, but so far there was no word from the police. No positive identification of the body. Nothing. Everything had gone quiet.

Santo's was an authentic Italian pizza parlor near the campus. Theo loved the place because there was always a crowd of students watching games on the big-screen TVs. The Boones and Whipples found a table and ordered two of "Santo's World-Famous Sicilian Pizzas." Theo didn't have the energy to ponder whether the pizza was indeed so famous. He had his doubts, just as he doubted the famousness of Gertrude's pecan waffles and Mr. Dudley's mint fudge. How could a town as small as Strattenburg have three dishes achieving the status of world recognition?

Theo let it go.

Stratten College had lost the game in the final minute, and it was the opinion of Mr. Boone that their coach had blundered badly by not managing his time-outs better. Mr. Whipple wasn't so sure, and a healthy discussion followed. Mrs. Boone and Mrs. Whipple, both busy lawyers, were soon tired of more basketball talk, and they launched into a private chat about the proposed renovation of the main courtroom. Theo was interested in both conversations and tried to follow them. Chase played a video game on his cell phone. Some fraternity boys began singing in a faraway corner. A crowd at the bar cheered the action on television.

Everyone seemed happy and not the least bit concerned about April.

Theo just wanted to go home.

## Chapter 11

Friday morning. After a crazy night of dreams, nightmares, frequent naps, insomnia, voices, and visions, Theo finally gave up and rolled out of bed at 6:30. As he sat on the edge of his bed and pondered what dreadful news the day would bring, he caught the unmistakable aroma of sausage drifting up from the kitchen. His mother prepared pancakes and sausage on those rare occasions when she thought her son and sometimes her husband needed a boost in the morning. But Theo wasn't hungry. He had no appetite and doubted if he would find one anytime soon. Judge, who slept under the bed, poked his head out and looked up at Theo. Both looked tired and sleepy.

"Sorry if I kept you awake, Judge," Theo said.

Judge accepted the apology.

"But then, you have the rest of the day to do nothing but sleep."

Judge seemed to agree.

Theo was tempted to flip open his laptop and check the local news, but he really didn't want to. Then he thought about grabbing the remote and turning on the television. Another bad idea. Instead, he took a long shower, got dressed, loaded his backpack, and was about to head downstairs when his cell phone rang. It was his uncle Ike.

"Hello," Theo said, somewhat surprised that Ike was awake at such an early hour. He was not known as a morning person.

"Theo, it's Ike. Good morning."

"Good morning, Ike." Though Ike was in his early sixties, he insisted that Theo call him simply Ike. None of that uncle stuff. Ike was a complicated person.

"What time are you headed to school?"

"Half an hour or so."

"You have time to run by and have a chat? I have some very interesting gossip that no one knows."

Theo was required by family ritual to stop by Ike's office every Monday afternoon. The visits usually lasted about thirty minutes and were not always pleasant. Ike liked to quiz Theo about his grades and his schoolwork and his future and so on, which was tedious. Ike was quick with a lecture. His own children were grown and lived far away, and Theo was his only nephew. He could not imagine why Ike wanted to see him so early on a Friday morning.

"Sure," Theo said.

"Hurry up, and don't tell anyone."

"You got it, Ike." Theo closed his phone and thought, How odd. But he had no time to dwell on it. And, his brain was already overloaded. Judge, no doubt because of the sausage, was scratching at the door.

Woods Boone had breakfast five days a week at the same table in the same downtown diner with the same group of friends at the same time, 7:00. Because of this, Theo rarely saw his father in the morning. Theo received a peck on the cheek from his mother, who was still in her robe, as they exchanged good morning and compared how they slept. Marcella, when she wasn't tied up in court, spent the early part of each Friday morning getting worked on. Hair, nails, toes. As a professional, she was serious about her appearance. Her husband was not quite as concerned about his.

"No news on April," Mrs. Boone said. The small television next to the microwave was not on.

"What does that mean?" Theo asked as he took a seat.

Judge was standing next to the stove, as close to the sausage as he could possibly get.

"It means nothing, at least for now," she said as she placed a plate in front of Theo. A stack of small round pancakes, three links of sausage. She poured him a glass of milk.

"Thanks, Mom. This is awesome. What about Judge?"

"Of course," she said as she placed a small plate in front of the dog. Pancakes and sausage, too.

"Dig in." She took her seat and looked at the large breakfast sitting in front of her son. She sipped her coffee. Theo had no choice but to eat like he was starving. After a few bites, he said, "Delicious, Mom."

"Thought you might need something extra this morning."

"Thanks."

After a pause in which she watched him closely, she said, "Theo, are you all right? I mean, I know this is just awful, but how are you handling it?"

It was easier to chew than to talk. Theo had no answer. How do you describe your emotions when a close friend is abducted and probably tossed in a river? How do you express your sadness when that friend was a neglected kid from a strange family with nutty parents, a kid who didn't have much of a chance?

Theo kept chewing. When he had to say something, he sort of grunted, "I'm okay, Mom." It was not the truth, but at the moment it was all he could manage.

"Do you want to talk about it?"

Ah, the perfect question. Theo shook his head and said, "No, I do not. That just makes it worse."

She smiled and said, "Okay, I understand."

Fifteen minutes later, Theo hopped on his bike, rubbed Judge's head, and said good-bye, then flew down the Boones' driveway and onto Mallard Lane.

Long before Theo was born, Ike Boone had been a lawyer. He had founded the firm with Theo's parents. The three lawyers worked well together and prospered, until Ike did something wrong. Something bad. Whatever Ike did, it was not discussed in Theo's presence. Naturally curious, and raised by two lawyers, Theo had been pecking away at Ike's mysterious downfall for several years, but he had learned little. His father rebuffed all nosiness with a brusque, "We'll discuss it when you get older." His mother usually said something like, "Your father will explain it one day."

Theo knew only the basics: (1) Ike had once been a smart and successful tax lawyer; (2) then he went to prison for several years; (3) he was disbarred and can never be a lawyer again; (4) while he was in prison, his wife divorced him and left Strattenburg with their three children; (5) the children, Theo's first cousins, were much older than Theo and he'd never met them; and (6) relations between Ike and Theo's parents were not that good.

Ike eked out a living as a tax accountant for small businesses and a few other clients. He lived alone in a tiny apartment. He liked to think of himself as a misfit, even a rebel against the establishment. He wore weird clothes, long, gray hair pulled into a ponytail, sandals (even in cold weather), and usually had the Grateful Dead or Bob Dylan playing on the cheap stereo in his office. He worked above a Greek deli, in a wonderfully shabby old room with rows of untouched books on the shelves.

Theo bounced up the stairs, knocked on the door as he pushed it open, and strolled into Ike's office as if he owned the place. Ike was at his desk, one even more cluttered than his brother Woods's, and he was sipping coffee from a tall paper cup. "Mornin', Theo," he said like a real grump.

"Hey, Ike." Theo fell into a rickety wooden chair by the desk. "What's up?"

Ike leaned forward on his elbows. His eyes were red and puffy. Over the years, Theo had heard snippets of gossip about Ike's drinking, and he assumed that was one reason his uncle got off to a slow start each morning.

"I guess you're worried about your friend, the Finnemore girl," Ike said.

Theo nodded.

"Well stop worrying. It ain't her. The body they pulled from the river appears to be that of a man, not a girl. They're not sure. DNA will confirm in a day or two, but the person is, or was, five feet six inches tall. Your friend was about five one, right?"

"I guess."

"The body is extremely decomposed, which suggests that it spent more than a few days in the water. Your friend was snatched late Tuesday night or early Wednesday morning. If her kidnapper tossed her in the river shortly after that, the body would not be as decomposed as this one. It's a mess, with a lot of missing parts. Probably been in the water for a week or so."

Theo absorbed this. He was stunned, relieved, and he couldn't suppress a grin. As Ike went on, Theo felt the tension ease in his chest and stomach.

"The police are going to make the announcement at nine this morning. I thought you might appreciate a little head start."

"Thanks, Ike."

"But they will not admit the obvious, and that is to

say that they've wasted the last two days with the theory that Jack Leeper took the girl, killed her, and tossed her in the river. Leeper is nothing but a lying thug, and the cops allowed themselves to chase the wrong man. This will not be mentioned by the police."

"Who told you all this?" Theo asked, and immediately knew it was the wrong question because it would not be answered.

Ike smiled, rubbed his red eyes, took a gulp of coffee, and said, "I have friends, Theo, and not the same friends I had years ago. My friends now are from a different part of town. They're not in the big buildings and fine homes. They're closer to the street."

Theo knew that Ike played a lot of poker, and his pals included some retired lawyers and policemen. Ike also liked to give the impression that he had a large circle of shady friends who watched everything from the shadows, and thus knew the street talk. There was some truth to this. The previous year, one of his clients was convicted for operating a small-time drug ring. Ike got his name in the paper when he was called to testify as the man's bookkeeper.

"I hear a lot of stuff, Theo," he added.

"Then who's the guy they pulled from the river?"

Another sip of coffee. "We'll probably never know. They've gone two hundred miles upriver and found no record of a missing person in the past month. You ever hear of the Bates's case?"

"No."

"Probably forty years ago."

"I'm thirteen years old, Ike."

"Right. Anyway, it happened over in Rooseburg. A crook named Bates faked his own death one night. Somehow snatched an unknown person, knocked him out, put this person in his car, a nice Cadillac, then ran it into a ditch and set it on fire. The police and firemen show up and the car is nothing but flames. They find a pile of cremated ashes and figure it's Mr. Bates. They have a funeral, a burial, the usual. Mrs. Bates collects the life insurance. Mr. Bates is forgotten until three years later when he's arrested in Montana outside a bar. They haul him back to face the music here. He pleads guilty. The big question is—who was the guy who got fried in his car? Mr. Bates says he doesn't know, never got the boy's name, just picked him up one night as a hitchhiker. Three hours later, the boy was reduced to ashes. Guess he got in the wrong car. Bates gets life in prison."

"What's the point here, Ike?"

"The point, my dear nephew, is that we may never know who the cops pulled from the river. There's a class of people out there, Theo—bums, drifters, hobos, homeless folk— who live in the underworld. They're nameless, faceless;

they move from town to town, hopping trains, hitchhiking, living in the woods and under the bridges. They've dropped out of society, and from time to time bad things happen to them. It's a rough and violent world they inhabit, and we rarely see them, because they do not wish to be seen. My guess is that the corpse the cops are inspecting will never be identified. But that's really not the point. The good news is that it's not your friend."

"Thanks, Ike. I don't know what else to say."

"I thought you might need some good news."

"It's very good news, Ike. I've been worried sick."

"She your girlfriend?"

"No, just a good friend. She has a weird family and I guess I'm one of the few kids she confides in."

"She's lucky to have a friend like you, Theo."

"Thanks, I guess."

Ike relaxed and put his feet on his desk. Sandals again, with bright red socks. He sipped his coffee and smiled at Theo. "How much do you know about her father?"

Theo squirmed and wasn't sure what to say. "I met him once, at their house. April's mother threw a birthday party for her a couple of years ago. It was a disaster because most of the kids didn't show up. The other parents didn't like the idea of them going to the Finnemores' house. But I was there, me and three others, and her dad was hanging around. He had long hair and a beard and seemed uncomfortable around us kids. April told me a lot over the years. He comes and goes and she's happier when he's not around. He plays the guitar and writes songs—bad songs according to April— and still has the dream of making it big as a musician."

"I know the guy," Ike said smugly. "Or, I should say, I know of him."

"How's that?" Theo asked, not really surprised that Ike knew another strange person.

"I have a friend who plays music with him occasionally, says he's a deadbeat. Spends a lot of time with a ragtag band of middle-aged losers. They take little tours, playing in bars and fraternity houses. I suspect there are some drugs involved."

"That sounds right. April told me he was missing one time for a whole month. I think he and Mrs. Finnemore fight a lot. It's a very unhappy family."

Ike slowly got to his feet and walked to the stereo mounted in a bookcase. He pushed a button, and some folk music began playing quietly in the background. Ike spoke as he fiddled with the volume, "Well, if you ask me, the police need to check out the father. He probably got the girl and took off somewhere."

"I'm not sure April would leave with him. She didn't like him and didn't trust him."

"Why hasn't she tried to contact you? Doesn't she have a cell phone, a laptop? Don't you kids chat nonstop online?"

"The police found her laptop in her room, and her parents would not allow her to have a cell phone. She told me once that her father hates cell phones and doesn't use one. He doesn't want to be found when he's on the road. I'm sure she would try and contact me if she could. Maybe whoever took her won't let her get near a phone."

Ike sat down again and looked at a notepad on his desk. Theo needed to get to school, which was ten minutes away by bike if he hit all the shortcuts.

"I'll see what I can find out about the father," Ike said. "Call me after school."

"Thanks, Ike. And, I suppose this is top secret, right, this great news about April?"

"Why should it be a secret? In about an hour the police will make the announcement. If you ask me, they should've informed the public last night. But, no, the police like to put on press conferences, make everything as dramatic as possible. I don't care who you tell. The public has the right to know."

"Great. I'll call Mom on the way to school."

# Chapter 12

Fifteen minutes later, Mr. Mount got his homeroom quiet and settled, which was not as difficult as usual. The boys were again subdued. There was a lot of gossip, but it was more of the whispered variety. Mr. Mount looked at them, and then said, gravely, "Men, Theo has an update on April's disappearance."

Theo stood slowly and walked to the front of the class. One of his favorite trial lawyers in town was a man named Jesse Meelbank. When Mr. Meelbank had a trial, Theo tried to watch as much as possible. The summer before, there was a long trial in which Mr. Meelbank sued a railroad company for the tragic death of a young woman, and Theo watched nonstop for nine days. It was awesome. What he loved about Mr. Meelbank was the way he carried himself in the courtroom. He moved gracefully, but with a purpose, never in a hurry but never wasting time. When he was ready to speak, he looked at the witness, or the judge or jury, and he paused dramatically before saying the first word. And when he spoke, his tone was friendly, conversational, seemingly off the cuff, but not a single word, phrase, or syllable was wasted. Everyone listened to Jesse Meelbank, and he seldom lost a case. Often, when Theo was alone in his bedroom or office (with the door locked), he liked to address the jury in some dramatic, make-believe case, and he always imitated Mr. Meelbank.

He stood before the class, paused just a second, and when he had everyone's attention, he said, "As we all know, the police found a dead body in the river yesterday. It was all over the news, and the reports suggested that the body was April Finnemore." (A dramatic pause as Theo searched their troubled eyes). "However, I have a reliable source that has confirmed that the body is not April. The body is that of a man about five feet six inches tall, and the poor guy has been in the water for a long time. His body is really decomposed."

Grins everywhere, on every face, even a clap or two.

Because he knew every lawyer, judge, court clerk, and practically every policeman in town, Theo's word carried great weight with his friends and classmates, at least in matters like this. When the topic was Chemistry, music, movies, or the Civil War, he was not the expert and did not pretend to be. But when it came to the law, the courts, and the criminal justice system, Theo was the man.

He continued, "At nine this morning, the police will make this announcement to the press. It's certainly good news, but the fact is, April is still missing and the police do not have many clues."

"What about Jack Leeper?" Aaron asked.

"He's still a suspect, but he's not cooperating."

The boys were suddenly talkative. They asked Theo more random questions, none of which he could answer, and they chatted among themselves. When the bell rang, they scampered off to first period, and Mr. Mount hustled down to the principal's office to repeat the good news. It spread like wildfire through the office and teachers' lounge, and then it spilled into the hallways and classrooms and even the restrooms and cafeteria.

A few minutes before 9:00 a.m., Mrs. Gladwell, the principal, interrupted the classes with an announcement through the intercom. All eighth-grade students were to report immediately to the auditorium for another unscheduled assembly. They had done the same thing the day before when Mrs. Gladwell tried to calm their fears.

As the students filed into the auditorium, a large television was being rolled in by two of the custodians. Mrs. Gladwell hurried everyone to their seats, and when they were seated, she said, "Attention, please!" She had an annoying way of dragging out the word *please* so that it sounded more like "Pleeeeeze." This was often imitated over lunch or on the playground, especially by the boys. Behind her, the screen came to life with a muted broadcast of a morning talk show. She went on, "At nine o'clock, the police are going to make an important announcement in the April Finnemore case, and I thought it would be great if we could see it live and enjoy this moment together. Pleeeeze, no questions."

She glanced at her watch, and then glanced at the television. "Let's put it on Channel twenty-eight," she said to the custodians. Strattenburg had two network stations and two cable. Channel 28 was arguably the most reliable, which meant that it generally made fewer blunders than the others. Theo had once watched a great trial in which Channel 28 was sued by a doctor who claimed a reporter for the station had said false things about him. The jury believed the doctor, as did Theo, and gave him a bunch of money.

Channel 28 was showing another morning talk show, one that started the hour not with the news but with the latest breathtaking details of a celebrity divorce. Thankfully, it was still on mute. The eighth graders waited patiently and quietly.

There was a clock on the wall, and when the minute hand made it to five minutes past nine, Theo began to squirm. Some of the students began to whisper. The celebrity divorce gave way to a bridal makeover, one in which a rather plain and somewhat chubby bride got worked on by all manner of flaky professionals. A trainer tried to whip her into shape by screaming at her. A man with painted fingernails restyled her hair. A real weirdo plastered on new makeup. This went on and on with virtually no improvement. By 9:15, the bride was ready for the wedding. She looked like a different person, and it was obvious, even with no sound, that her groom preferred the version he had originally proposed to.

But by then, Theo was too nervous to care. Mr. Mount eased over to him and whispered, "Theo, are you sure the police will make the announcement?"

Theo nodded confidently and said, "Yes, sir."

But all confidence had vanished. Theo was kicking

himself for being such a loudmouth and know-it-all. He was also kicking Ike. He was tempted to sneak his cell phone out of his pocket and text Ike to see what was going on. What were the police doing? The school, though, had a strict policy regarding cell phones. Only seventh and eighth graders could have them on campus, and calls, texts, and e-mails were permitted only during lunch and recess. If you got caught using your phone at any other time, then you lost your phone. About half of the eighth graders had cell phones. Many parents still refused to allow them.

"Hey, Theo, what's the deal?" Aaron Helleberg asked at full volume. He was seated behind Theo, three seats down.

Theo smiled, shrugged, and said, "These things never run on time."

Once the chubby bride got married, it was time for the morning news. Floods in India were claiming thousands of lives, and London got hit with a freak snowstorm. With the news out of the way, one of the hosts began an exclusive interview with a supermodel.

Theo felt as though every teacher and every student was staring at him. He was anxious and breathing rapidly, and then he had an even worse thought. What if Ike was wrong? What if Ike had believed some bad information and the police were not so sure about the dead body?

Wouldn't Theo look like an idiot? Indeed he would, but that would be nothing if the police had in fact pulled April out of the water.

He jumped to his feet and walked over to where Mr. Mount was standing with two other teachers. "I've got an idea," he said, still managing to appear confident. "Why don't you call the police department and see what's going on?" Theo said.

"Who would I call?" Mr. Mount asked.

"I'll give you the number," Theo said.

Mrs. Gladwell was walking over, frowning at Theo.

"Why don't you call, Theo?" Mr. Mount said, and that was exactly what Theo wanted to hear. He looked at Mrs. Gladwell and said, very politely, "May I step into the hall and call the police department?"

Mrs. Gladwell was pretty nervous about the situation, too, and she quickly said, "Yes, and hurry."

Theo disappeared. In the hall, he whipped out his cell phone and called Ike. No answer. He called the police department, but the line was busy. He called Elsa at the office and asked if she had heard anything. She had not. He tried Ike again, no answer. He tried to think of someone else to call at that awful moment, but no one came to mind. He checked the time on his cell phone—9:27.

Theo stared at the large metal door that led into the auditorium where about 175 of his classmates and a dozen or so teachers were waiting on some very good news about April, news that Theo had brought to school and delivered as dramatically as possible. He knew he should open the door and return to his seat. He thought about leaving, just going someplace in the school and hiding for an hour or so. He could claim that his stomach was upset, or that his asthma had flared up. He could hide in the library or the gym.

The doorknob clicked and Theo stuck the phone to his ear as if in a deep conversation. Mr. Mount came out, looked at him quizzically, and mouthed the words "Is everything okay?" Theo smiled and nodded his head as if he had the police on the line and they were doing exactly what he wanted them to do. Mr. Mount returned to the auditorium.

Theo could (1) run and hide; (2) stop the damage with a little fib, something like—"The announcement by the police has been postponed," or (3) stick with the current plan and pray for a miracle. He thought about throwing rocks at Ike, then gritted his teeth, and pulled open the door. Everyone watched him as he returned. Mrs. Gladwell pounced on him. "What's going on, Theo?" she said, eyebrows arched, eyes flashing.

"It should be any minute now," he said.

"Who did you talk to?" Mr. Mount asked—a rather direct question.

"They're having some technical problems," Theo replied, dodging. "Just a few more minutes."

Mr. Mount frowned as if he found this hard to believe. Theo quickly got to his seat and tried to become invisible. He focused on the television screen, where a dog was gripping two paintbrushes in his teeth and splashing paint on a white canvas while the host howled with laughter. Come on, Theo said to himself, someone save me here. It was 9:35.

"Hey, Theo, any more inside scoop?" Aaron said loudly, and several kids laughed.

"At least we're not in class," Theo shot back.

Ten more minutes passed. The painting dog gave way to an obese chef who built a pyramid out of mushrooms, then almost cried when it all tumbled down. Mrs. Gladwell walked in front of the television, shot a vicious look at Theo, and said, "Well, you need to get back to class."

At that moment, Channel 28 cut in with a BREAKING NEWS graphic. A custodian hit the mute switch, and Mrs. Gladwell hurried out of the way. Theo exhaled and thanked God for miracles.

The Police Chief was behind a podium with a row of uniformed officers behind him. To the far right was Detective Slater in a coat and tie. Everyone looked exhausted.

The chief read from a page of notes, and he gave the same information Ike had delivered to Theo about two hours earlier. They were waiting on DNA testing to confirm things, but they were almost certain the body pulled from the river was not that of April Finnemore. He went into some detail about the size and condition of the body, which they were working hard to identify, and he gave the impression they were making progress. As for April, they were following many leads. The reporters asked a lot of questions, and the chief did a lot of talking, but not much was said.

When the press conference was over, the eighth graders were relieved, but still worried. The police had no idea where April was, or who took her. Jack Leeper was still the prime suspect. At least she wasn't dead, or if she was, they didn't yet know it.

As they left the auditorium and returned to class, Theo reminded himself to be more cautious next time. He had just barely avoided being the biggest laughingstock in school.

During the lunch break, Theo, Woody, Chase, Aaron, and a few others ate sandwiches and talked about resuming their search after school. The weather, though, was threatening and heavy rain was predicted for the afternoon and into the night. As the days had dragged by, there were fewer and fewer among them who believed April was still in Strattenburg. Why, then, should they search the streets each afternoon if no one believed she would be found?

Theo was determined to continue, rain or not.

# Chapter 13

Halfway through Chemistry, with rain and wind pounding the windows, Theo was trying to listen to Mr. Tubcheck when he was startled to hear his own name. It was Mrs. Gladwell again, over the intercom. "Mr. Tubcheck, is Theodore Boone in class?" she screeched, startling the boys and Mr. Tubcheck as well.

Theo's heart stopped as he bolted straight up in his chair. Where else would I be at this moment? he thought.

"He is," Mr. Tubcheck responded.

"Please send him to the office."

As Theo walked slowly down the hall, he tried desperately to think of why he was needed in the principal's office. It was almost 2:00 p.m. on Friday afternoon. The week was almost over, and what a miserable week it had been. Perhaps Mrs. Gladwell was still sore over the delayed press conference this morning, but Theo didn't think so. That had turned out well. He had done nothing significantly wrong the entire week, violated no rules, offended no one, successfully completed most of his homework, and so on. He gave up. He really wasn't that worried. Two years earlier, Mrs. Gladwell's oldest daughter had gone through an unpleasant divorce, and Marcella Boone had been her lawyer.

Miss Gloria, the nosy receptionist, was on the phone and waved him toward the big office. Mrs. Gladwell met him at the door and escorted him inside. "Theo, this is Anton," she said as she closed the door. Anton was a skinny kid with extremely dark skin. She continued, "He's in Miss Spence's sixth-grade class." Theo shook his hand and said, "Nice to meet you."

Anton said nothing. His handshake was rather limp. Theo immediately thought the kid was in deep trouble and scared to death.

"Have a seat, Theo," she said, and Theo fell into the chair next to Anton. "Anton is from Haiti, moved here several years ago, and lives with some relatives at the edge of town on Barkley Street, near the quarry." Her eyes met Theo's when she said the word *quarry*. It was not a better part of town. In fact, most of the people who lived there were low income or immigrants, legal and otherwise.

"His parents are working out of town, and Anton lives with his grandparents. Do you recognize this?" she asked as she handed Theo a sheet of paper. He studied it quickly, and said, "Oh boy."

"Are you familiar with Animal Court, Theo?" she asked.

"Yes, I've been there several times. I rescued my dog from Animal Court."

"Can you please explain what's going on, for my benefit and Anton's?"

"Sure. This is a Rule 3 Summons, issued by Judge Yeck from Animal Court. Says here that Pete was taken into custody yesterday by Animal Control."

"They came to the house and got him," Anton said. "Said he was under arrest. Pete was very upset."

Theo was still scanning the summons. "Says here that Pete is an African gray parrot, age unknown."

"He's fifty years old. He's been in my family for many years."

Theo glanced at Anton and noticed his wet eyes.

"The hearing is today at 4:00 p.m. in Animal Court. Judge Yeck will hear the case and decide what to do with Pete. Do you know what Pete did wrong?"

"He scared some people," Anton said. "That's all I know."

"Can you help, Theo?" Mrs. Gladwell asked.

"Sure," Theo said, with some reluctance. Truthfully, though, Theo loved Animal Court because anyone, including a thirteen-year-old kid in the eighth grade, could represent himself or herself. Lawyers were not required in Animal Court, and Judge Yeck ran a very loose courtroom. Yeck was a misfit who'd been kicked out of several law firms, couldn't handle a real job as a lawyer, and was not too happy to be the lowest-ranked judge in town. Most lawyers avoided "Kitty Court," as it was known, because it was beneath their dignity.

"Thank you, Theo."

"But I need to leave now," he said, thinking quickly. "I need some time to prepare."

"You're dismissed," she said.

At 4:00 p.m., Theo walked down the stairs to the basement level of the courthouse, and down a hallway past storage rooms until he came to a wooden door with ANIMAL COURT, JUDGE SERGIO YECK, stenciled in black at the top. He was nervous, but also excited. Where else could a thirteen-year-old argue a case and pretend to be a real lawyer? He was carrying a leather briefcase, one of Ike's old ones. He opened the door.

Whatever Pete had done, he'd done a good job of it. Theo had never seen so many people in Animal Court. On the left side of the small courtroom, there was a group of women, all middle-aged, all wearing tight, brown riding britches and black leather boots up to their knees. They looked very unhappy. To the right, sitting as far away from the women as possible, were Anton and two elderly black people. All three appeared to be terrified. Theo eased over to them and said hello. Anton introduced his grandparents, with names that were foreign and impossible to understand the first time around. Their English was okay, but heavily accented. Anton said something to his grandmother. She looked at Theo and said, "You our lawyer?"

Theo couldn't think of anything else to say but, "Yes."

She started crying.

A door opened and Judge Yeck appeared from somewhere in the rear. He stepped up to the long bench and sat down. As usual, he was wearing jeans, cowboy boots, no tie, and a battered sports coat. No black robe was needed in Kitty Court. He picked up a sheet of paper and glanced around the room. Few of the cases on his docket attracted attention. Most involved people whose dogs and cats had been picked up by Animal Control. So, when a little controversy came his way, he enjoyed the moment.

He cleared his throat loudly and said, "I see here that we have a case involving Pete the Parrot. His owners are Mr. and Mrs. Regnier." He looked at the Haitians for confirmation. Theo said, "Your Honor, I'm with the, uh, the owners."

"Well, hello, Theo. How are you doing these days?"

"Fine, Judge, thanks."

"I haven't seen you in a month or so."

"Yes, sir, I've been busy. You know, classes and all."

"How are your folks?"

"Fine, just fine."

Theo had first appeared in Animal Court two years earlier when he made a last-minute plea to save the life of a mutt no one wanted. He took the dog home and named him Judge.

"Please come forward," Judge Yeck said, and Theo led the three Regniers through the small gate to a table on the right. When they were seated, the judge said, "The complaint was filed by Kate Spangler and Judy Cross, owners of SC Stables."

A well-dressed young man popped up and announced, "Yes, Your Honor, I represent Ms. Spangler and Ms. Cross."

"And who are you?"

"I'm Kevin Blaze, Your Honor, with the Macklin firm." Blaze sort of strutted up to the bench, shiny new briefcase in hand, and placed one of his business cards in front of the judge. The Macklin firm was a group of about twenty lawyers and had been around for years. Theo had never heard of Mr. Blaze. Evidently, Judge Yeck had not either. It was apparent, at least to Theo, that the young lawyer's abundance of self-confidence was not appreciated.

Theo suddenly had a sharp pain in his midsection. His opponent was a real lawyer!

Blaze got his clients, the two women, properly seated at the table on the left side of the courtroom, and when everyone was in place, Judge Yeck said, "Say, Theo, you don't happen to own any part of this parrot do you?"

"No, sir."

"Then why are you here?"

Theo stayed in his chair. In Animal Court, all formalities were dispensed with. The lawyers remained seated. There was no witness stand, no sworn oaths to tell the truth, no rules of evidence, and certainly no jury. Judge Yeck conducted quick hearings and ruled on the spot, and in spite of his dead-end job, he was known to be fair.

"Well, uh," Theo began badly. "You see, Your Honor, Anton goes to my school, and his family is from Haiti, and they don't understand our system."

"Who does?" Yeck mumbled.

"And I guess I'm here as a favor to a friend."

"I get that, Theo, but normally the owner of the pet shows up to argue his or her case or they hire a lawyer. You're not the owner, and you're not a lawyer, yet."

"Yes, sir."

Kevin Blaze jumped to his feet and said sharply, "I object to his presence here, Your Honor."

Judge Yeck slowly turned his attention from Theo and settled it heavily onto the eager face of young Kevin Blaze. There was a long pause; a tense lull in the proceedings in which no one spoke and no one seemed to breathe. Finally, Judge Yeck said, "Sit down."

When Blaze was back in his seat, Judge Yeck said, "And stay there. Don't get up again unless I ask you to. Now, Mr. Blaze, can you not see that I am addressing the issue of Theodore Boone's presence in this matter? Is that not obvious to you? I need no assistance from you. Your objection is useless. It is not overruled, nor is it sustained. It is simply ignored." Another long pause as Judge Yeck looked at the group of women seated behind the table on the left.

He pointed and asked, "Who are these people?"

Blaze, firmly gripping the arms of his chair, said, "These are witnesses, Your Honor."

Judge Yeck was obviously not happy with this response.

"Okay, here's the way I operate, Mr. Blaze. I prefer short hearings. I prefer few witnesses. And I really have no patience with witnesses who say the same things that other witnesses have already said. You understand this, Mr. Blaze?"

"Yes, sir."

Looking at Theo, the judge said, "Thank you for taking an interest in this case, Mr. Boone."

"You're welcome, Judge."

His Honor glanced at a sheet of paper and said, "Good. Now, I suppose we need to meet Pete." He nodded to his ancient court clerk, who disappeared for a moment then returned with a uniformed bailiff holding a cheap, wire birdcage. He placed it on the corner of Judge Yeck's bench. Inside the cage was Pete, an African gray parrot, fourteen inches long from beak to tail. Pete glanced around the strange room, moving only his head.

"I guess you're Pete," Judge Yeck said.

"I'm Pete," Pete said in a clear, high-pitched voice.

"Nice to meet you. I'm Judge Yeck."

"Yeck, Yeck, Yeck," Pete squawked, and almost everyone laughed. The ladies in the black boots did not. They were frowning even harder now, not at all amused by Pete.

Judge Yeck exhaled slowly, as if the hearing might take longer than he wanted. "Call your first witness," he said to Kevin Blaze.

"Yes, Your Honor. I guess we'll start with Kate Spangler."
Blaze reshifted his weight and turned to look at his client.
It was obvious he wanted to stand and move around the
courtroom, and felt constrained. He picked up a legal pad
covered with notes, and began, "You are the co-owner of SC
Stables, correct?"

"Yes." Ms. Spangler was a small, thin woman in her mid-
forties.

"How long have you owned SC Stables?"

"Why is that important?" Judge Yeck interrupted
quickly. "Please tell me how that is possibly relevant to what
we're doing here."

Blaze tried to explain. "Well, Your Honor, we need to
prove that—"

"Here's how we do things in Animal Court, Mr. Blaze.
Ms. Spangler, please tell me what happened. Just forget all
the stuff your lawyer has told you, and tell me what Pete
here did to upset you."

"I'm Pete," Pete said.

"Yes, we know."

"Yeck, Yeck, Yeck."

"Thank you, Pete." A long pause to make sure Pete
was finished for the moment, then the judge waved at Ms.
Spangler. She began, "Well, on Tuesday of last week, we were
in the middle of a lesson. I was in the arena, on foot, with

four of my students mounted, when suddenly this bird here came out of nowhere, squawking and making all kinds of noises, just a few feet above our heads. The horses freaked out and bolted for the barn. I almost got trampled. Betty Slocum fell and hurt her arm."

Betty Slocum stood quickly so everyone could see the large, white cast on her left arm.

"He swooped down again, like some crazy kamikaze, and chased the horses as they—"

"Kamikaze, kamikaze, kamikaze," Pete blurted.

"Just shut up!" Ms. Spangler said to Pete.

"Please, he's just a bird," Judge Yeck said.

Pete began saying something that could not be understood. Anton leaned over and whispered to Theo. "He's speaking Creole."

"What is it?" Judge Yeck asked.

"He's speaking Creole French, Your Honor," Theo explained. "It's his native tongue."

"What's he saying?"

Theo whispered to Anton, who whispered right back. "You don't want to know, Your Honor," Theo reported.

Pete shut up, and everyone waited for a moment. Judge Yeck looked at Anton and said softly, "Will he stop talking if he's asked to stop talking?"

Anton shook his head and said, "No, sir."

Another pause. "Please continue," Judge Yeck said.

Judy Cross took over and said, "And then the next day, at about the same time, I was giving a lesson. I had five of my riders on their horses. In the course of any lesson, I yell instructions to my students, such as 'Walk on,' and 'Halt,' and 'Canter.' I had no idea he was watching us, but he was. He was hiding in an oak tree next to the arena, and he started yelling, "'Halt! Halt!'"

Pete, on cue, yelled, "Halt! Halt! Halt!"

"See what I mean? And the horses stopped dead still. I tried to ignore him. I told my students to remain calm and just ignore this guy. I said 'Walk on,' and the horses began their movements. Then he started yelling, "'Halt!' 'Halt!'"

Judge Yeck held up both hands for silence. Seconds passed. He said, "Please continue."

Judy Cross said, "He was quiet for a few minutes. We ignored him. The students were concentrating and the horses were calm. They were in a slow walk, when suddenly he started yelling, 'Canter! Canter!' The horses bolted again and began sprinting all around the arena. It was chaos. I barely escaped getting run over."

Pete squawked, "Canter! Canter!"

"See what I mean," Judy Cross gushed. "He's been

harassing us for over a week. One day he'll drop from the sky like a dive-bomber and frighten the horses. The next day he'll sneak up on us and hide in a tree and wait until things are quiet before he starts yelling instructions. He's evil. Our horses are afraid to come out of the barn. Our students want their money back. He's killing our business."

With perfect timing, Pete said, "You're fat."

He waited five seconds, then did it again. "You're fat." His words echoed around the room and stunned everyone. Most of the people looked at their shoes, or boots.

Judy Cross swallowed hard, closed her eyes tightly, clenched her fists, and frowned as if in great pain. She was a large woman with a wide frame, the kind of body that had always carried extra weight, and carried it badly. It was obvious from her reaction that her weight had presented many complicated issues over the years. It was something she had battled, and lost badly. Being heavy was an extremely sensitive topic for Judy, one she wrestled with every day.

"You're fat," Pete reminded her, for the third time.

Judge Yeck, who was desperately fighting the natural reaction to burst out laughing, jumped in and said, "Okay. Is it safe to assume that your other witnesses are willing to say pretty much the same thing?" The women nodded. Several seemed to be cowering, almost hiding, as if they had lost some of their enthusiasm. At that moment, it would take enormous courage to say harmful things about Pete. What would he blurt out about them, and their bodies?

"Anything else?" Judge Yeck asked.

Kate Spangler said, "Judge, you've got to do something. This bird is costing us our business. We've already lost money. This simply isn't fair."

"What do you want me to do?"

"I don't care what you do. Can you put him to sleep or something?"

"You want me to kill him?"

"Halt! Halt!" Pete screamed.

"Maybe you could clip his wings," Judy Cross chimed in.

"Halt! Halt!" Pete continued, then he resorted to Creole and unleashed a furious string of harsh words at the two women. When he finished, Judge Yeck glanced at Anton and asked, "What did he say?"

Anton's grandparents were chuckling and covering their mouths.

"Really bad stuff," Anton replied. "He doesn't like those two women."

"Got that." The judge raised his hands again and asked for calm. Pete got the message. "Mr. Boone."

Theo said, "Well, Judge, I think it might be helpful if my friend Anton gave you some background on Pete."

"Please do so."

Anton cleared his throat, and began nervously. "Yes, sir. Pete is fifty years old. He was given to my father when he was a little boy in Haiti, a gift from his father, so Pete has been in the family for a long time. When my grandparents came to this country a few years ago, Pete came, too. African gray parrots are some of the smartest animals in the world. As you can see, he knows a lot of words. He understands what others are saying. He can even imitate the voices of humans."

Pete was watching Anton as he spoke, the voice so familiar. He began saying, "Andy, Andy, Andy."

"I'm here, Pete," Anton said.

"Andy, Andy."

A pause, then Anton continued, "Parrots like to have a fixed routine each day, and they require at least an hour out of their cages. Every day at four o'clock, Pete gets out, and we thought he was just hanging around the backyard. I guess not. The stables are about a mile away, and he must have found the place. We're very sorry about this, but please don't hurt Pete."

"Thank you," Judge Yeck said. "Now, Mr. Blaze, what am I supposed to do?"

"Your Honor, it's obvious that the owners cannot control this bird, and it's their duty to do so. One compromise might be that the court orders the owners to have its wings clipped. I've checked with two veterinarians and one wildlife specialist, and they've told me that such a procedure is not unusual, nor is it painful or expensive."

At full volume, Pete yelled, "You're stupid."

There was laughter as Blaze's face turned red. Judge Yeck said, "Okay that's enough. Get him out of here. Pete, sorry old boy, but you must leave the room." The bailiff snatched the birdcage and took him away. As the door closed, Pete was cursing mightily in Creole.

When the room was quiet again, Judge Yeck said, "Mr. Boone, what's your suggestion?"

With no hesitation, Theo said, "Probation, Your Honor. Give us one more chance. My friends here will find a way to control Pete and keep him away from the stables. I don't think they realize what he's been doing, or the problems he's created. They are very sorry for all this."

"And if he does it again?"

"Then a harsher punishment would be in order." Theo knew two things that Kevin Blaze did not. First, Judge Yeck believed in second chances and rarely ordered animals destroyed until he had no other choice. Second, he'd been kicked out of the Macklin law firm five years earlier, so he probably held a bit of a grudge.

In typical Yeck fashion, he said, "Here's what we're going to do. Ms. Spangler and Ms. Cross, I am very sympathetic to your complaints. If Pete shows up again, I want you to video him. Have a cell phone or a camera ready, and catch him on video. Then bring me the video. At that point, Mr. Boone, we will take Pete into custody and have his wings clipped. The owners will be responsible for the costs. There will be no hearing—it will be automatic. Is this clear, Mr. Boone?"

"Just a second, Your Honor." Theo huddled with the three Regniers and they were soon nodding in agreement.

"They understand, Your Honor," Theo announced.

"Good. I hold them responsible. I want Pete kept at home. Period."

"Can they take him home now?" Theo asked.

"Yes. I'm sure the good folks at the animal shelter are ready to get rid of him. Case closed. Court's adjourned."

Kevin Blaze and his clients and the rest of the women in black boots hustled out of the courtroom. When they were gone, the bailiff brought Pete back and handed him over to Anton, who immediately opened the cage and removed the bird. His grandparents wiped tears from their cheeks as they stroked his back and tail.

Theo drifted away and walked to the bench where Judge Yeck was making notes on his docket. "Thanks, Judge," Theo said, almost in a whisper.

"That's a bad bird," Judge Yeck said softly with a chuckle. "Too bad we don't have a video of Pete dive-bombing the ladies on their horses." They both laughed, but quietly.

"Nice job, Theo."

"Thanks."

"Any word on the Finnemore girl?"

Theo shook his head. No.

"I'm very sorry, Theo. Someone told me you're a close friend."

Theo nodded and said, "Pretty close."

"Let's keep our fingers crossed."

"Yeck, Yeck, Yeck," Pete squawked as he left the court-room.

# Chapter 14

Jack Leeper wanted to talk. He sent a note to the jailer, who passed it on to Detective Slater. Late Friday afternoon, they marched Leeper from his cell block and through an old tunnel which led to the police station next door. Slater and his trusty sidekick, Capshaw, were waiting in the same dim and cramped interrogation room. Leeper looked as though he had not bathed or shaved since they had chatted with him the day before.

"Something on your mind, Leeper." Slater began rudely. As always, Capshaw was taking notes.

"I talked to my lawyer today," Leeper said, as if he were now more important because he had a lawyer.

"Which one?"

"Ozgoode, Kip Ozgoode."

As if they had rehearsed, both detectives chuckled and sneered at the name. "If you have Ozgoode, you're dead meat, Leeper," Slater said.

"The worst," Capshaw added.

"I like him," Leeper said. "He seems a lot smarter than you boys."

"You want to talk or swap insults?"

"I can do both."

"Does your lawyer know you're talking to us?" Slater asked.

"Yep."

"So what do you want to talk about?"

"I'm worried about the girl. You clowns obviously can't find her. I know where she is, and as the clock ticks her situation gets worse. She needs to be rescued."

"You're a real sweetheart, Leeper," Slater said. "Snatch the girl, stash her somewhere, and now you want to help her."

"I'm sure you have a deal for us," Capshaw said.

"You got it. Here's what I'll do, and you guys better do it fast because there's one frightened little girl out there. I'll plead guilty to one count of breaking and entering;

get two years in prison, with my time to run at the same time as that mess in California. I stay here and do my time. My lawyer says the paperwork can be done in a matter of hours. We sign the deal, the prosecutor and judge okay it, and you get the girl. Time is crucial here boys, so you'd better make a move."

Slater and Capshaw exchanged a nervous look. Leeper had them. They suspected he was lying because they expected nothing else from him. But what if he wasn't? What if they agreed to his deal and he led them to April?

Slater said, "It's almost six p.m. on Friday afternoon, Leeper. All the judges and prosecutors have gone home."

"Oh, I'll bet you can find them. They'll hustle up if there's a chance of saving the girl."

Another pause as they studied his bearded face. Why would he offer such a deal if he didn't know where she was? Such a plea bargain would be thrown out the window if he couldn't deliver. Plus, they had no other leads, no other suspects. Leeper had always been their man.

"I don't mind having a chat with the prosecutor," Slater said, giving in.

"If you're lying, Leeper, we'll ship you back to California come Monday," Capshaw said.

"Is she still in town?" Slater asked.

"I'm not saying another word until I sign the deal," Leeper said.

As Theo was leaving the courthouse after saving Pete the Parrot, he saw a text message from Ike, who wanted him to run by the office.

Because he got off to a slow start each day, Ike usually worked late, even on Fridays. Theo found him at his desk, piles of papers everywhere, a bottle of beer already opened, and Bob Dylan on the stereo.

"How's my favorite nephew?" Ike said.

"I'm your only nephew," Theo replied as he shook off his raincoat and sat in the only chair that wasn't covered with files and binders.

"Yes, but Theo you'd be my favorite even if I had twenty."

"If you say so."

"How was your day?"

Theo had already learned that a large part of being a lawyer was relishing the victories, especially the ones involving courtroom battles. Lawyers love to tell stories about their weird clients and strange cases, but they thrive on their dramatic wins in court. So Theo launched into the saga of Pete, and before long Ike was roaring with laughter. Not surprisingly, Judge Yeck did not hang out with the more respected lawyers in town, and he and Ike occasionally bumped into one another at a certain bar where some of the misfits liked to drink. Ike thought it was hilarious that Yeck allowed Theo to handle cases like a real lawyer.

When the story was over, Ike changed subjects and said, "I still say the police should be checking out the girl's father. From what I hear, they're still concentrating on Jack Leeper, and I think that's a mistake. Don't you?"

"I don't know, Ike. I don't know what to think."

Ike picked up a piece of paper. "His name is Thomas Finnemore, goes by Tom. His band calls itself Plunder and they've been on the road for a few weeks. Finnemore and four other clowns, most from around here. There's no website. The lead singer is a former drug dealer I met years ago, and I managed to track down one of his current girlfriends. She wouldn't say much, but she thinks they're in the Raleigh, North Carolina, area doing cheap gigs in bars and fraternity houses. She did not act as though she missed her boyfriend that much. Anyway, that's all I could find out."

"So what am I supposed to do?"

"See if you can find Plunder."

Theo shook his head in frustration. "Look, Ike, there's no way April would take off with her father. I've tried to tell you. She doesn't trust him, and she really dislikes him."

"And she was scared, Theo. A very frightened little girl.

You don't know what she was thinking. Her mother had abandoned her. These people are nuts, right?"

"Right."

"No one broke in the house, because her father has a key. He gets her and they take off, for how long no one knows."

"Okay, but if she's with her father, then she's safe, right?"

"You tell me. You think she's safe hanging around with Plunder? Not the best place for a thirteen-year-old girl."

"So I find Plunder, and just hop on my bike and fly down to Raleigh, North Carolina."

"We'll worry about that later. You're a whiz with a computer. Start searching, see what you can find."

What a waste of time, Theo thought. He was suddenly tired. The week had been stressful and he'd slept little. The excitement of Animal Court had sapped whatever energy he had, and he just wanted to go home and crawl into bed.

"Thanks, Ike," he said as he grabbed his raincoat.

"Don't mention it."


Late Friday night, Jack Leeper was once again handcuffed and led from his cell. The meeting took place in a room at the jail where lawyers met with their clients. Leeper's lawyer, Kip Ozgoode, was there, along with Detectives Slater and Capshaw, and a young lady from the prosecutor's office named Teresa Knox. Ms. Knox immediately took charge.

She was all business and didn't appreciate being called from home on a Friday night.

"There's no deal, Mr. Leeper," she began. "You're in no position to make deals. You're facing kidnapping charges, which means up to forty years in prison. If the girl is harmed, then more charges. If she's dead, then your life is really over. The best thing for you is to tell us where she is so she won't be harmed anymore and you won't face additional charges."

Leeper grinned at Ms. Knox but said nothing.

She continued, "This is assuming, of course, that you're not playing games. I suspect that you are. So does the judge. So do the police."

"Then all of you will be sorry," Leeper said. "I'm giving you the chance to save her life. As for me, I'm sure I'll die in prison."

"Not necessarily," Ms. Knox fired back. "You give us the girl, safe and sound, and we'll recommend a twenty-year sentence on the kidnapping charge. You can serve your time here."

"What about California?"

"We can't control what they do in California."

Leeper kept grinning, as if he was enjoying the moment. Finally, he said, "As you say, no deal."

# Chapter 15

The Boone family breakfast on Saturday morning was rather tense. As usual, Theo and Judge dined on Cheerios—orange juice for Theo but not for Judge—while Woods Boone ate a bagel and read the sports page. Marcella sipped coffee and scanned her laptop for news around the world. Not much was said, at least not for the first twenty minutes. The remains of other conversations were still hanging in the air, and a disagreement might flare up at any moment.

The tension had several causes. First, and most obvious, was the general gloominess that had afflicted the family since about 4:00 a.m. Wednesday morning when they were awakened by the police and asked to hurry over to the Finnemore home. As the days passed without April, the mood had only darkened. There were efforts, especially by Mr. and Mrs. Boone, to smile and be upbeat, but all three knew these were futile. Second, but less important, was the fact that Theo and his father would not play their weekly nine holes of golf. They teed off almost every Saturday at 9:00 a.m., and it was the highlight of the week.

The golf was being cancelled because of the third reason for the tension. Mr. and Mrs. Boone were leaving town for twenty-four hours, and Theo insisted he be allowed to stay by himself. It was a fight they'd had before, and Theo had lost before, and he was losing again. He had carefully explained that he knew how to lock all the doors and windows; arm the alarm system; call the neighbors and 911, if necessary; sleep with a chair wedged under his door; sleep with Judge by his side ready to attack, and sleep with a seven-iron golf club in his grip, if necessary. He was thoroughly and completely safe and he resented being treated like a child. He refused to stay with a babysitter when his parents went out for dinner or the movies, and he was furious that they refused to leave him on this little overnight trip of theirs.

His parents wouldn't budge. He was only thirteen and that was too young to be left alone. Theo had already started the negotiating, even pestering, and the door was open to serious discussion on the issue when he was fourteen. But for now, Theo needed the supervision and protection. His mother had arranged for him to spend the night with Chase Whipple, which would have been okay under normal circumstances. However, as Chase had explained, his own parents were going out for dinner Saturday night and leaving the two boys to be watched by Chase's older sister, Daphne, a truly dislikable girl of sixteen who was always at home because she had no social life and therefore felt compelled to flirt with Theo. He had suffered through such a sleepover not three months earlier when his parents were in Chicago for a funeral.

He had protested, griped, sulked, argued, pouted, and nothing had worked. His Saturday night was about to be spent in the basement of the Whipple home with pudgy Daphne chattering nonstop and staring at him while he and Chase tried to play video games and watch television.

Mr. and Mrs. Boone had considered cancelling their trip, in light of April's abduction and the general sense of uneasiness in town. Their plans were to drive two hundred miles to a popular resort called Briar Springs for a few hours of fun with a bunch of lawyers from around the state. There would be afternoon seminars and speeches, then cocktails, then a long dinner with more speeches from wise old judges and dull politicians. Woods and Marcella were active in the State Bar Association and never missed the annual meeting at Briar Springs. This one was even more important because Marcella was scheduled to give a speech on recent trends in divorce law, and Woods was on tap to participate in a seminar on the mortgage foreclosure crisis. Both had prepared their remarks and were looking forward to the afternoon.

Theo assured them he would be fine, and that Strattenburg would not miss them if they left for twenty-four hours. Over dinner Friday evening, they had decided to make the trip. And they had decided that Theo would stay with the Whipple family, in spite of his vocal opposition to such a plan. Theo lost the argument, and though he conceded this to himself he still awoke on Saturday in a foul mood.

"Sorry about the golf, Theo," Mr. Boone said without taking his eyes off the sports page.

Theo said nothing.

"We'll catch up next Saturday by playing eighteen. Whatta you say?"

Theo grunted.

His mother closed her laptop and looked at him. "Theo,

dear, we're leaving in an hour. What are your plans for the afternoon?"

Seconds passed before Theo said, "Oh, I don't know. I guess I'll just hang out here and wait for the kidnappers and murderers to show up. I'll probably be dead by the time you get to Briar Springs."

"Don't get smart with your mother," Woods said sharply, then raised the newspaper to conceal a grin.

"You'll have a great time at the Whipples," she said.

"Can't wait."

"Now, back to my question. What are your plans for the afternoon?"

"Not sure. Chase and I might go the high school game at two, or we might go to the Paramount and watch the double feature. There's also a hockey game."

"And you're not searching for April, right, Theo? We've had this conversation. You boys have no business riding around town playing detectives."

Theo nodded.

His father lowered his newspaper, glared at Theo, and said, "Do we have your word, Theo? No more search parties?"

"You have my word."

"I want a text message every two hours, beginning at eleven this morning. Do you understand?" his mother asked.

"I do."

"And smile, Theo. Make the world a happier place."

"I don't want to smile right now."

"Come on, Teddy," she said with a smile of her own. Calling him Teddy did nothing to brighten his mood, nor did her constant reminders to "smile and make the world a happier place." Theo's thick braces had been stuck to his teeth for two years and he was sick of them. He could not imagine how a blazing mouth full of metal could possibly make anyone happier.

They left at 10:00 a.m. on the dot, on schedule, because they planned to arrive precisely at 1:30 p.m. Marcella's speech was at 2:30 p.m.; Woods's seminar was at 3:30 p.m. As busy lawyers, their lives revolved around the clock, and time could not be wasted.

Theo waited half an hour, then loaded up his backpack and took off to the office. Judge followed him. As expected, Boone & Boone was deserted. His parents rarely worked on Saturday, and the staff certainly did not. He unlocked the front door, disarmed the alarm system, and switched on the lights to the main library near the front of the building. Its tall windows looked onto the small front lawn, then the street. The room had the look and smell of a very important room, and Theo often did his homework there, if the lawyers and paralegals weren't using it. He fixed Judge a bowl of water, and then unpacked his laptop and cell phone.

He'd spent a couple of hours the night before searching for Plunder. He still found it hard to believe that April would leave in the middle of the night with her father, but Ike's theory was better than anything Theo could come up with. Besides, what else did Theo have to do over the weekend?

So far, there was no sign of Plunder. Working in the Raleigh-Durham-Chapel Hill area, Theo had found dozens of music halls, clubs, private party rooms, concert venues, bars and lounges, even wedding receptions. About half had websites or Facebook pages, and not one had mentioned a band called Plunder. He also found three underground weeklies that listed hundreds of possible venues for live music.

Using the office landline, Theo began cold calling, in alphabetical order. The first was a joint called Abbey's Irish Rose in Durham. A scratchy voice said, "Abbey's."

Theo tried to lower his voice as much as possible. "Yes, could you tell me if the band Plunder is playing there tonight?"

"Never heard of 'em."

"Thanks." He hung up quickly.

At Brady's Barbeque in Raleigh, a woman said, "We don't have a band tonight."

Theo, with every question scripted to learn as much as possible, asked, "Has Plunder ever played there?"

"Never heard of 'em."

"Thanks."

He plowed on, chewing up the alphabet, getting nowhere. There was a decent chance that Elsa would question the phone calls when she opened the monthly bill, and if this happened Theo would take the blame. He might even warn Elsa, tell her why he made the calls, and ask her to pay the bill without telling his parents. He would deal with it later. He had no choice but to use the office phone because his mother was a Nazi about his cell phone bill. If she saw a bunch of calls to a bunch of bars in Raleigh-Durham, he would have some explaining to do.

The first whiff of success came from a place called Traction in Chapel Hill. A helpful young man, who sounded no older than Theo, said he thought that Plunder had played there a few months earlier. He put Theo on hold and went to check with someone named Eddie. When it was confirmed that Plunder had passed through, the young man said, "You're not thinking about booking them, are you?"

"Maybe," Theo replied.

"Don't. They can't draw flies."

"Thanks."

"It's a frat band."

At exactly 11:00 a.m., he texted his mother: *Home alone. Serial killer in basement.*

She replied: *Not funny. Love you.*

*Love u.*

Theo plugged away, call after call, with little trace of Plunder.

Chase arrived around noon and unpacked his laptop. By then, Theo had chatted with over sixty managers, bartenders, waitresses, bouncers, even a dishwasher who spoke very little English. His brief conversations convinced him that Plunder was a bad band with a very small following. One bartender in Raleigh, who claimed to "know every band that ever came to town," admitted he'd never heard of Plunder. On three occasions, the band was referred to as a "frat band."

"Let's check out the fraternities," Chase said. "And the sororities, too."

They soon learned that there were a lot of colleges and universities in the Raleigh-Durham area, with the obvious being Duke, UNC, and NC State. But within an hour's drive, there were a dozen smaller schools. They decided to start with the larger ones. Minutes passed as the two pecked away, flying around the Internet, racing to be the first to find something useful. "Duke doesn't have fraternity houses," Chase said.

"What does that mean, in terms of parties and bands?" Theo asked.

"I'm not sure. Let's come back to Duke. You take NC State and I'll take UNC."

Theo soon learned that NC State had twenty-four fraternities and nine sororities, most with an off-campus house as headquarters. It appeared as though each maintained a website, though they varied in quality. "How many frats at UNC?" Theo asked.

"Twenty-two for the boys and nine for the girls."

"Let's go through each website."

"That's what I'm doing." Chase's fingers never stopped moving. Theo was quick with his laptop, but not as quick as Chase. The two raced on, each determined to dig up the first bit of useful intelligence. Judge, who always preferred to sleep under things—tables, beds, chairs—snored quietly somewhere under the conference table.

The websites soon blurred together. They provided information on members, alumni, service projects, awards, calendars, and, most importantly, social events. The photos were endless—party scenes, ski trips, cookouts on the beach, Frisbee tournaments, and formals with the boys in tuxedos and the girls in fancy dresses. Theo caught himself looking forward to college.

The two schools played each other in football, with

kickoff at 2:00 p.m. Theo knew this; in fact, he and Chase had discussed the line. NC State was a two-point favorite. Now, though, the line was not that interesting. The important part of the game was that it gave the fraternities another excuse to party. The game was in Chapel Hill, so evidently the State students had partied and danced on Friday night. The UNC fraternities and sororities were planning the same for Saturday night.

Theo closed another website and grunted in frustration. "I count ten frat parties last night at State, but only four websites give the names of the bands. If you're announcing a party on your website, why wouldn't you say who's going to be playing?"

"Same here," Chase said. "They rarely give the name of the band."

"How many parties in Chapel Hill tonight?" Theo asked.

"Maybe a dozen. Looks like a big night."

They finished the search of all websites at both schools. It was 1:00 p.m.

Theo texted his mother: *With Chase. Ax murderers in hot pursuit. Won't make it. Please take care of Judge. Love.*

A few minutes later she replied: *So nice to hear from you. Be safe. Love Mom.*

# Chapter 16

Theo found a bag of pretzels and two diet drinks in the small kitchen where the Boone & Boone firm waged quiet battles over food. The rules were simple: If you brought food that was not to be shared, then put your initials on it and hope for the best. Otherwise, everything was fair game. Reality, though, was more complicated. The "borrowing" of food from someone's private stash was commonplace, and not entirely frowned upon. Courtesy demanded that if food was borrowed, it should be replaced as soon as possible. This led to all sorts of pranks. Mr. Boone referred to the kitchen as a "minefield" and refused to go near it.

Theo suspected the pretzels and drinks belonged to

Dorothy, a secretary who was eternally trying to lose weight. He made a mental note to replenish her supply.

Chase had suggested they go to the high school at 2:00 p.m. to watch Strattenburg play its first basketball game of the season, and Theo agreed. He was tired of the Internet and considered their work useless. But he had one last idea. "Since the parties were at State last night, let's go through each fraternity there, do a random check of several Facebook pages, and look at photos."

"You said there were ten parties, right?" Chase was crunching on a thick pretzel.

"Yes, with four giving the name of the band. That leaves six parties with unknown bands."

"And what, exactly, are we looking for?"

"Anything that might identify Plunder. Electric lights, a banner, the band's name on the bass drum, anything."

"So what if we find out that the band played at a frat party last night at NC State? Does that mean they're playing tonight at UNC?"

"Maybe. Look, Chase, we're just guessing here, all right? We're throwing darts in the dark."

"You got that right."

"You have a better idea?"

"Not at the moment."

Theo sent Chase the links to three fraternities. "Sigma Nu has eighty members," Chase said. "How many—"

"Let's do five from each fraternity. Pick them at random. Of course, you'll have to use pages with open profiles and no security."

"I know, I know."

Theo went to the page of a Chi Psi member named Buddy Ziles, a sophomore from Atlanta. Buddy had a lot of friends and hundreds of photos, but nothing from a party the night before. Theo plowed ahead, as did Chase, with little being said. Both boys were soon bored by the endless shots of groups of students posing, yelling, dancing, always with a beer in hand.

Chase perked up and said, "I got some shots from last night. A party with a band." He went through the photos, slowly, and then said, "Nothing."

A hundred photos later, Theo stopped cold, blinked twice, and zoomed in. He was on the unsecured Facebook page of an Alpha Nu brother named Vince Snyder, a sophomore from D.C. who had posted a dozen photos from last night's dance. "Chase, come here," Theo said, as if he were watching a ghost.

Chase scurried around behind Theo and leaned in. Theo pointed to the screen. The photo was a typical party shot with a mob of kids dancing. "You see that?" he said.

"Yes, what is it?"

"It's a Minnesota Twins jacket, navy with red-and-white lettering."

In the center was a small dance floor, and whoever took the photo did so with the intent of capturing some friends as they moved to the music. One girl in particular had a very short skirt, and Theo figured that was the reason for the photo. To the left of the dance floor, almost in the middle of the mob, was the lead singer, holding a guitar, mouth open, eyes closed, wailing away, and just beyond him was the point where Theo was pointing. Behind a set of tall speakers, there was a small person who appeared to be watching the crowd. The person was standing sideways, and only the *T* and *W* of the word *TWINS* were visible across the back of the jacket. The person had short hair, and though most of her face was lost in the shadows, there was no doubt in Theo's mind.

It was April.

And as of 11:39 p.m., the time of the photo, she was very much alive.

"Are you sure?" Chase asked, leaning closer, their noses almost touching the screen.

"I gave her that Twins jacket last year after I won it in a contest. It was too small for me. I told the police about it and they said they never found it in her house. They assume she was wearing it when she left." Theo pointed again and said, "Look at the short hair and the profile, Chase, it's gotta be April. Don't you agree?"

"Maybe. I don't know."

"It's her," Theo said. Both boys backed away, and then Theo stood up and walked around the room. "Her mother had not been home for three straight nights. She was scared to death, so she called her father, or maybe he called her. Anyway, he drove through the night, got home, unlocked the door with his key, got April, and away they went. For the past four days she's been on the road, just hanging out with the band."

"Shouldn't we call the police?"

Theo was walking, pacing, thinking, rubbing his chin as he pondered the situation. "No, not yet. Maybe later. Let's do this—since we know where she was last night, let's try and figure out where she'll be tonight. Let's call every fraternity and sorority at UNC, Duke, Wake Forest, and the rest of them until we find out where Plunder is playing tonight."

"UNC is the hot spot," Chase said. "There are at least a dozen frat parties."

"Give me the list."

Theo worked the phone as Chase watched and took notes. At the first fraternity house, no one answered the phone. The second call was to the Kappa Delta sorority house, and the young lady who answered the phone was not sure what their band's name was. The third call went unanswered. At the Delta house, a brother gave the name of another band. And on it went. Theo was growing frustrated again, but he was also thrilled to know that April had not been harmed and he was determined to find her.

The eighth call was magic. A student at the Kappa Theta fraternity house said he knew nothing about a band, was late for the football game, but to hang on a minute. He returned to the phone and said, "Yep, it's a band called Plunder."

"What time do they start playing," Theo asked.

"Whenever. Usually around nine. Gotta run, pal."

The pretzels were gone. The truth was that Theo had no idea what to do. Chase felt strongly that they should call the police, but Theo wasn't so sure.

Two things were certain, at least to Theo. One, the girl in the photo was April. Two, she was with the band and the band would be playing at the Kappa Theta house in Chapel Hill, North Carolina, that night. Instead of calling the police, Theo called Ike.

Twenty minutes later, Theo, Chase, and Judge ran up the stairs to Ike's office. He had been eating lunch in the Greek deli downstairs when Theo called. He and Chase introduced themselves as Theo found the photo of April on Ike's desktop computer.

"That's her," Theo declared. Ike studied the photo carefully, his reading glasses perched on the tip of his nose. "Are you sure?"

Theo gave the history of the jacket. He described her height, hairstyle, and hair color, and pointed at the profile of her nose and chin. "That's April," he said.

"If you say so."

"She's with her father, just like you said, Ike. Jack Leeper had nothing to do with her disappearance. The police have been chasing the wrong man."

Ike nodded and smiled but was not the least bit smug. He continued to stare at his computer screen.

"Chase thinks we should notify the police," Theo said.

"I sure do," Chase said. "Why not?"

"Let me think about it," Ike said as he pushed back his chair and jumped to his feet. He turned on his stereo and walked around the office. Finally, he said, "I don't like the idea of notifying the police, at least not right now. Here's what might happen. The police here would call the police in Chapel Hill, and we're not sure what they would do down there. They would probably go to the party and try and find April. This might be more difficult than you think. Let's assume it's a large party, with lots of students celebrating and drinking and other stuff and anything might happen when the police show up. The police might be smart; maybe they're not. Maybe they have no interest in a girl who's just hanging around while her father plays in a band. Maybe the girl doesn't want to be rescued by the police. A lot of things might happen, and most of them not good. There's no warrant out for the arrest of her father because the police here haven't charged him with anything. He's not a suspect, yet." Ike paced along behind his desk as the boys watched every move and hung on every word. "And without a positive identification, I'm not sure the police here would do anything in the first place."

He fell into his chair and stared at the photo. He frowned, pinched his nose, and rubbed his whiskers.

"I know it's her," Theo said.

"But what if it isn't, Theo?" Ike said gravely. "There's more than one Twins jacket in the world. You can't see her eyes. You know it's April because you really want it to be April. You're desperate for it to be April, but what if you're wrong? Let's say we go to the police right now, and they get excited and call their buddies down in Chapel Hill, who also get excited, and tonight they go to the party and (a) can't find the girl, or (b) find the girl and it's not April. We'd look pretty stupid, wouldn't we?"

There was a long heavy pause as the boys considered

how stupid they would look if they were wrong. Finally, Chase spoke. "Why don't we tell her mother? I'll bet she could identify her own daughter, then it's out of our hands."

"I don't think so," Ike said. "That woman's crazy and she might do anything. It's not in April's best interests to have her mother involved at this point. From what I hear, she's driving the police crazy and they're trying to avoid her."

Another long pause as all three looked at the walls. Theo said, "So what do we do, Ike?"

"The smartest thing to do is to go get the girl, bring her back, then call the police. And it has to be done by someone she trusts, someone like you, Theo."

Theo's jaw dropped, his mouth flew open, but no words came out.

"That's a long bike ride," Chase said.

"Tell your parents, Theo, and get them to drive you down there. You have to confront April, make sure she's okay, and bring her back. Immediately. There's no time to waste."

"My parents aren't here, Ike. They're in Briar Springs for the state bar convention and won't be back until tomorrow. I'm staying with Chase tonight."

Ike looked at Chase and asked, "Could your parents make the trip?"

Chase was already shaking his head. "No, I don't think

so. I can't see them getting involved in something like this. Besides, they're having dinner with some friends tonight and it's a big deal."

Theo looked at his uncle and saw in his eyes the unmistakable twinkle of a kid ready for an adventure. "Looks like you're the man, Ike," Theo said. "And, as you say, there's no time to waste."

# Chapter 17

The adventure immediately faced some serious problems. Theo thought about his parents and whether or not he should tell them. Ike thought about his car and knew it couldn't make the trip. Chase thought about the fact that Theo was supposed to spend the night at his house, and it seemed impossible that his absence would go unnoticed.

As for his parents, Theo did not like the idea of calling them and asking permission to take off to Chapel Hill. Ike thought this was a good plan—Chase was neutral—but Theo resisted. Such a call would ruin their trip, upset their speeches and seminars, and so on, and, besides, Theo figured his parents (especially his mother) would say no. Then he would be faced with the decision to obey, or not. Ike thought he could smooth things out and convince Woods and Marcella that the trip was urgent, but Theo wouldn't budge. He believed in being honest with his parents and he concealed little from them, but this was different. If they brought April back, then everyone, including his parents, would be so thrilled that Theo would likely avoid trouble.

Ike's car was a Triumph Spitfire, a notoriously unreliable old sports car with only two seats, a convertible roof that leaked, tires that were nearly bald, and an engine that made strange sounds. Theo loved the car but often wondered how it managed to putter around town. And, they needed four seats—Ike, Theo, Judge, and hopefully, April. His parents had left in his mother's car. His father's SUV was in the garage, ready to go. Ike decided he could borrow the vehicle from his own brother, especially in light of the importance of their mission.

The most serious problem would be Chase's. He would have to hide Theo's absence from the Whipple home throughout the night. They discussed the possibility of informing Chase's parents. Ike even volunteered to call them and explain what they were doing, but Theo thought it was a bad idea. Mrs. Whipple was a lawyer, too, and had plenty to say about almost everything, and there was no doubt in Theo's mind that she would immediately call his mother and ruin their plans. There was another reason Theo wanted Ike to stay quiet—Ike's reputation among lawyers was not good. Theo could easily imagine Mrs. Whipple freaking out at the thought of Ike Boone racing off with his nephew on some crazy road trip.

At 3:00 p.m., Theo texted his mother: *Still alive. With Chase. Hanging out. Luv.*

Theo expected no response because at that moment his mother was in the middle of her presentation.

At 3:15, Theo and Chase parked their bikes in the Whipple driveway and went inside. Mrs. Whipple was pulling a tray of brownies from the oven. She threw her arms around Theo, welcomed him to their home, said she was so happy to have him as a guest, and so on. She tended to be overly dramatic. Theo sat his red Nike overnight bag on the table, so she couldn't miss it.

As she served them brownies and milk, Chase said they were thinking about going to the movies, then maybe watching the volleyball game at Stratten College.

"Volleyball?" Mrs. Whipple asked.

"I love volleyball," Chase said. "The game starts at six

and should be over around eight. We'll be fine, Mom. It's just at the college."

In truth, the volleyball game was the only sports event on campus that evening. And girls' volleyball at that. Neither Chase nor Theo had ever watched a game, live or on TV.

"What's on at the movies?" she asked, still cutting brownies into squares.

"*Harry Potter*," Theo said. "If we hustle now, we can catch most of it."

Chase chimed in, "And then we'll go to the game. Is that okay, Mom?"

"I suppose," she said.

"Are you and Dad still going out for dinner?"

"Yes, with the Coleys and the Shepherds."

"What time will you be home?" Chase asked, glancing at Theo.

"Oh, I don't know. Ten or ten thirty. Daphne will be here and she wants to order a pizza. Is that okay?"

"Sure," Chase said. With a little luck, Theo and Ike should be in Chapel Hill by 10:00 p.m. The tricky part would be avoiding Daphne from eight until ten. Chase didn't have a plan, but he was working on it.

They thanked her for the snack and said they were leaving for the Paramount, Strattenburg's old-fashioned movie house on Main Street. After they were gone, Mrs. Whipple carried Theo's overnight bag upstairs to Chase's room and placed it on a twin bed.

At 4:00 p.m., Theo, Ike, and Judge left the Boone home in the SUV. Chase was watching the latest Harry Potter, alone.

MapQuest estimated the travel time at seven hours if one obeyed all speed limits, which was the furthest thing from Ike's mind. As they hurried out of town, Ike said, "Are you nervous?"

"Yes, I'm nervous."

"And why are you nervous?"

"I guess I'm nervous about getting caught. If Mrs. Whipple finds out, then she'll call my mother and my mother will call me and I'm in big trouble."

"Why would you get in trouble, Theo? You're trying to help a friend."

"I'm being dishonest, Ike. Dishonest with the Whipples, dishonest with my parents."

"Look at the big picture, Theo. If all goes well, tomorrow morning we'll be back home with April. Your parents, and everyone else in town, will be thrilled to see her. Under the circumstances, this is the right thing to do. It might be a little misleading, but there's no other way to do it."

"It still makes me nervous."

"I'm your uncle, Theo. What's wrong with me and my favorite nephew taking a little road trip?"

"Nothing, I guess."

"Then stop worrying. The only thing that matters is finding April, and getting her back home. Nothing else is important right now. If it all blows up, I'll have a little chat with your parents and I'll take all the blame. Relax."

"Thanks, Ike."

They were racing down the highway in light traffic. Judge was already asleep on the backseat. Theo's phone vibrated. It was a text from Chase: *This movie is awesome. U guys OK?*

Theo responded: *Yep. OK.*

At 5:00 p.m., he texted his mother: *Harry Potter movie is awesome.*

A few minutes later she answered, *Great. Love Mom.*

They turned onto the expressway, and Ike set the cruise control on seventy-five, ten miles over the limit.

Theo said, "Explain something to me, Ike. The story about April has been all over the news, right?"

"Right."

"Then, wouldn't April or her father or one of the guys in the band see the story on the news and realize what's going on? Wouldn't they know about the big search for April?"

"You would think so. Unfortunately, though, there are a lot of missing children, seems like a new one every other day. And while it's big news around here, maybe it's not big news where they are. Who knows what her father has told his pals in the band. I'm sure they know the family is not too stable. Maybe he's told them that the mother is crazy and he was forced to rescue his daughter, and that he wants it kept quiet until some point in the future. The band members might be afraid to say anything. These guys are not too stable either. It's a bunch of forty-year-old men trying to be rock stars, up all night, sleeping all day, traveling around in a rented van, playing for peanuts in bars and frat houses. They're probably all running from something. I don't know, Theo, it makes no sense."

"I'll bet she's scared to death."

"Scared, and confused. A child deserves better than this."

"What if she doesn't want to leave her father?"

"If we find her, and she refuses to come with us, then we have no choice but to call the police in Strattenburg and tell them where she is. It's that simple."

Nothing seemed simple to Theo. "What if her father sees us and causes trouble?"

"Just relax, Theo. It'll work out."

It was dark at 6:30 when Chase texted again: *Vball girls r cute. Where R U?*

Theo answered: *Somewhere n Virginia. Ike's flying.*

It was dark now, and the hectic week finally caught up with Theo. He began to nod off, and then fell into a deep sleep.

# Chapter 18

Late in the volleyball game, Chase realized that the only way to avoid Daphne was to avoid his house altogether. He could almost see her sitting in the family room in the basement, watching the big-screen TV, waiting for him and Theo to arrive so she could order an extra-large pizza from Santo's.

When the game was over, Chase rode his bike to Guff's Frozen Yogurt near the city library on Main Street. He ordered one scoop of banana, found an empty booth by the front window, and called home. Daphne answered after the first ring.

"It's me," he said. "And look, we have a problem. Theo

and I stopped by his house to check on his dog, and the dog is real sick. Must've eaten something weird. Throwing up, crapping all over the place; the house is a mess."

"Gross," Daphne gushed.

"You wouldn't believe. Dog poop from the kitchen to the bedroom. We're cleaning up now but it'll take some time. Theo's afraid the dog might be dying, and he's trying to get in touch with his mother."

"That's awful."

"Yep. We may have to take him to the vet emergency room. Poor thing can hardly move."

"Can I help, Chase? I can drive Mom's car over and get him."

"Maybe, but not right now. We gotta get this place cleaned up while we're watching the dog. I'm afraid he'd make a mess in her car."

"Have you guys eaten?"

"No, and food is the last thing we're thinking about right now. I'm about to throw up myself. Go ahead and order the pizza. I'll check in later." Chase hung up and smiled at his frozen yogurt. So far so good.

Judge was still asleep on the rear seat, snoring softly as the miles flew by. Theo came and went, napping occasionally, wide-eyed one moment and dead to the world the next. He was awake when they crossed the state line into North Carolina, but he was asleep when they rolled into Chapel Hill.

His 9:00 p.m. text to his mother read: *Going to sleep. Real tired. Luv.*

He assumed his parents were in the middle of their long dinner, probably listening to endless speeches, and that his mother would not have the chance to reply. He was right.

"Wake up, Theo," Ike said. "We're here." They had not stopped in six hours. The digital clock on the dash gave the time at 10:05. The GPS above it took them straight to Franklin Street, the main drag that bordered the campus. The sidewalks were packed with noisy students and fans. UNC had won the football game in overtime and the mood was rowdy. The bars and shops were crowded. Ike turned onto Columbia Street and they passed some large fraternity houses.

"Parking might be a problem," Ike mumbled, almost to himself. "That must be Frat Court," he said, glancing at the GPS and pointing to an area where several fraternity houses faced each other with parking lots in the center. "I'd guess the Kappa Theta house is somewhere in there."

Theo lowered his window as they eased by in heavy

traffic. Loud music filled the air as several bands played from the houses. People were shoulder-to-shoulder, on the porches, on the lawns, sitting on cars, hanging out, dancing, laughing, moving in packs from house to house, yelling at each other. It was a wild scene, and Theo had never seen anything like it. There was an occasional fight or drug bust at Stratten College, but nothing like this. It was exciting at first, but then Theo thought about April. She was somewhere in the midst of this huge carnival, and she did not belong here. She was shy and quiet and preferred to be alone with her drawings and paintings.

Ike turned onto another street, then another. "We'll have to park somewhere and hike in." Cars were parked everywhere, most illegally. They found a spot on a dark narrow street, far away from the noise. "Stay here, Judge," Theo said, and Judge watched them walk away.

"What's the game plan, Ike?" Theo asked. They were walking quickly along a dark and uneven sidewalk.

"Watch your step," Ike said. "We don't have a game plan. Let's find the house, find the band, and I'll think of something." They followed the noise and were soon entering Frat Court from the back side, away from the street. They moved into the crowd, and if they looked a bit odd, no one seemed to notice—a sixty-two-year-old man with long, gray hair pulled into a ponytail, red socks, sandals, a brown plaid sweater that was at least thirty years old, and a thirteen-year-old kid wide-eyed in amazement.

The Kappa Theta house was a large, white stone structure with some Greek columns and a sweeping porch. Ike and Theo made their way through a thick crowd, up the steps, and around the porch. Ike wanted to scope out the place, check out the entrances and exits, and try to determine where the band was playing. The music was loud, the laughter and yelling even louder. Theo had never seen so many cans of beer in his young life. Girls were dancing on the porch as their dates watched them and smoked cigarettes. Ike asked one of the girls, "Where's the band?"

"In the basement," she said.

They inched their way back to the front steps and looked around. The front door was being guarded by a large young man in a suit who seemed to have the authority to decide who got inside.

"Let's go," Ike said. Theo followed him as they moved toward the front door with a group of students. They almost made it. The guard, or bouncer, or whatever he was, threw out his arm and grabbed Ike by the forearm. "Excuse me!" he said rudely. "You got a pass?"

Ike angrily yanked his arm away and looked as though he might slug the guy. "I don't need a pass, kid," he hissed.

"I'm the manager of the band. This is my son. Don't touch me again."

The other students moved back a few steps and for a moment things were quieter.

"Sorry, sir," the guard said, and Ike and Theo marched inside. Ike was moving quickly, as though he knew the house well and had business there. They walked through a large foyer, then a parlor of some sort, both rooms crowded with students. In another open space, a mob of male students was yelling at a football game on a huge screen, two kegs of beer close by. The music was booming from below, and they soon found a large stairway that gave way to the party room. The dance floor was in the center, packed with students engaged in all manner of frenzied jerking and shuffling, and to the left was Plunder, pounding and screeching at full volume. Ike and Theo drifted down in a throng of people, and by the time they left the stairs, Theo felt like his ears were bleeding from the music.

They tried to hide in a corner. The room was dark, with colored strobe lights flickering across the mass of bodies. Ike leaned down and yelled into Theo's ear. "Let's be quick. I'll stay here. You try and get behind the band and have a look. Hurry."

Theo ducked low and wiggled around bodies. He got bumped, shoved, almost stepped on, but he kept moving along the wall on the far left side. The band finished a song, everybody cheered, and for a moment the dancing stopped. He moved faster, still low, his eyes darting in all directions. Suddenly, the lead singer screamed, then began howling. The drummer attacked and a guitarist lurched in with some thunderous chords. The next song was even louder. Theo passed a set of large speakers, came within five feet of the keyboardist, and then saw April, sitting on a metal box behind the drummer. She had the only safe place in the entire room. He practically crawled around the edge of the small platform and touched her knee before she saw him.

April was too shocked to move, then both hands flew up to her mouth. "Theo!" she said, but he could barely hear her. "Let's go!" he demanded.

"What are you doing here?" she yelled.

"I'm here to take you home."

At 10:30, Chase was hiding beside a dry cleaners, watching from across the street as people were leaving Robilio's Italian Bistro. He saw Mr. and Mrs. Shepherd, then Mr. and Mrs. Coley, then his parents. He watched them drive away, and then wondered what to do next. His phone would ring in a few minutes, and his mother would have a dozen questions. The sick dog routine was about to come to an end.

# Chapter 19

Theo and April inched along the wall, sidestepping weary dancers taking a break from the action, and moved quickly through the semidarkness to a door that opened onto a stairway. There was no chance her father would see them, because he was lost in Plunder's intense version of the Rolling Stones' "I Can't Get No Satisfaction."

"Where are we going?" Theo yelled at April.

"This leads outside," she yelled back.

"Wait! I gotta get Ike."

"Who?"

Theo darted through the crowd, found Ike where he'd left him, and the three made a quick exit down the stairs and onto a small patio behind the Kappa Theta house. The music could still be heard and the walls seemed to vibrate, but things were much quieter outside.

"Ike, this is April," Theo said. "April, this is Ike, my uncle."

"My pleasure," Ike said. April was still too confused to respond. They were alone, in the dark, beside a broken picnic table. Other patio furniture was strewn about. Windows on the back side of the house were broken.

Theo said, "Ike drove me down here to get you."

"But why?" she asked.

"What do you mean, 'Why'?" Theo shot back.

Ike understood her confusion. He took a step forward and gently placed a hand on her shoulder. "April, back home no one knows where you are. No one knows if you're dead or alive. Four days ago you vanished without a trace. No one—including your mother, the police, your friends—has heard a word from you."

April began shaking her head in disbelief.

Ike continued: "I suspect your father has been lying to you. He's probably told you that he's talked to your mother and everything is okay back home, right?"

April nodded slightly.

"He's lying, April. Your mother is worried sick. The

entire town has been searching for you. It's time to go home, now."

"But we were going home in just a few days," she said.

"According to your father?" Ike said, patting her shoulder. "There's a good chance he will face criminal charges for your abduction. April, look at me." Ike placed a finger under her chin and slowly lifted it so that she had no choice but to look at him. "It's time to go home. Let's get in the car and leave. Now."

The door opened and a man appeared. With biker boots, tattoos, and greasy hair, he was obviously not a student. "What are you doing, April?" he demanded.

"Just taking a break," she said.

He stepped closer and asked, "Who are these guys?"

"Who are you?" Ike demanded. Plunder was in the middle of a song, so he obviously wasn't a member of the band.

"He's Zack," April said. "He works for the band."

Immediately, Ike saw the danger and came through with some fiction. He reached out with a big handshake and said, "I'm Jack Ford, my son Max, here. We used to live in Strattenburg, now we're in Chapel Hill. Max and April started kindergarten together. Quite a band you got in there."

Zack shook hands. He was too slow to put together his

thoughts. He frowned, as if thinking caused pain, then he gave Ike and Theo a puzzled look. April said, "We're almost finished. I'll be just a minute."

"Does your dad know these guys?" Zack asked.

"Oh sure," Ike said. "Tom and I go back many years. I'd like to talk to him during the next break, if you could pass that along, Zack."

"Okay, I guess," Zack said, and went inside.

"Will he tell your father?" Ike asked.

"Probably," she said.

"Then we should leave, April."

"I don't know."

"Come on, April," Theo said firmly.

"Do you trust Theo?" Ike asked.

"Of course."

"Then you can trust Ike," Theo said. "Let's go."

Theo grabbed her hand and they began walking quickly away from the Kappa Theta house, from Frat Court, and from Tom Finnemore.

April sat in the backseat with Judge and rubbed his head as Ike zigzagged his way out of Chapel Hill. Nothing was said for a few minutes, then Theo asked, "Should we call Chase?"

"Yes," Ike said. They pulled into an all-night gas station

and parked away from the pumps. "Dial him," Ike said. Theo did so and handed the phone to Ike.

Chase answered his cell phone immediately with, "It's about time."

"Chase, this is Ike. We have April and we're headed back. Where are you?"

"Hiding in my backyard. My parents are ready to kill me."

"Go in the house and tell them the truth. I'll call them in about ten minutes."

"Thanks, Ike."

Ike handed the phone to Theo and asked, "Which of your parents is more likely to answer their cell phone at this time of the night?"

"My mom."

"Then get her on the phone." Theo punched the number and handed it back to Ike.

Mrs. Boone answered with a nervous, "Theo. What's the matter?"

Ike calmly said, "Marcella, this is Ike. How are you doing?"

"Ike? On Theo's phone? Why am I suddenly worried?"

"It's a very long story, Marcella, but no one is hurt. Everybody's fine, and there's a happy ending."

"Please, Ike. What's going on?"

"We have April."

"You what?"

"We have April and we're driving back to Strattenburg."

"Where are you, Ike?"

"Chapel Hill, North Carolina."

"Keep talking."

"Theo found her, and we took a little road trip to get her. She's been with her father the entire time, sort of hanging out."

"Theo found April in Chapel Hill?" Mrs. Boone repeated slowly.

"Yep. Again, it's a long story and we'll fill in the details later. We'll be home early in the morning, I'd guess between six and seven. That is, if I can stay awake all night and drive."

"Does her mother know?"

"Not yet. I was thinking that she should call her mom, tell her what's up."

"Yes, Ike, and the sooner the better. We'll check out now and drive home. We'll be there when you get there."

"Great, Marcella. And, I'm sure we'll be starving."

"Got it, Ike."

They passed the phone back and forth again, and Ike spoke to Mr. Whipple. He explained the situation, assured him everything was fine, heaped praise on Chase for helping find April, apologized for the deception and confusion, and promised to check in later.

Ike pulled over to the pumps, filled the tank, and when he went inside to pay, Theo took Judge for a quick walk. When they were on the road again, Ike said over his shoulder, "April, do you want to call your mother?"

"I guess," she said.

Theo handed her his cell phone. She tried her house, but there was no answer. She tried her mother's mobile, and there was no service.

"What a surprise," April said. "She's not there."

# Chapter 20

Ike had a tall cup of coffee, which he gulped down in an effort to stay awake. Just a few miles out of town, he said, "Okay, kids, here's the deal. It's midnight. We have a long way to go, and I'm already sleepy. Talk to me. I want chatter. If I fall asleep at the wheel, we all die. Understand? Go, Theo. You talk, then, April, it's your turn."

Theo turned and looked at April. "Who is Jack Leeper?"

April had Judge's head in her lap. She answered, "A distant cousin, I think. Why? Who told you about him?"

"He's in Strattenburg, in jail. He escaped from prison in California a week or so ago, and he showed up in town about the time you disappeared."

"His face has been all over the newspapers," Ike said.

"The police thought he snatched you and took off," Theo added.

Back and forth they went, tag-teaming as they told Leeper's story; his mug shots on the front page, his dramatic capture by the SWAT team, his vague threats about hiding April's body, and so on. April, who was overwhelmed by the events of the past hour, seemed unable to digest the entire story. "I've never met him," she mumbled softly, over and over.

Ike slurped his coffee and said, "The newspaper said you wrote him letters. You guys were pen pals. That right?"

"Yes. About a year ago we started writing," she said. "My mother said we are distant cousins, though I could never find him in our family tree. It's not your normal family tree. Anyway, she said he was serving a long sentence in California, and was looking for a pen pal. I wrote him, he wrote back. It was kind of fun. He seemed to be very lonely."

Ike said, "They found your letters in his cell after he escaped. He showed up in Strattenburg, so the police assumed he came after you."

"I can't believe this," she said. "My father told me he talked to my mom, and that he talked to the people at the school, and that everyone agreed that I would be gone for a week or so. No problem. I should've known better."

"Your father must be a pretty good liar," Ike said.

"He's one of the best," April said. "He's never told me the truth. I don't know why I believed him this time."

"You were scared, April," Theo said.

"Omigosh!" she said. "It's midnight. The band is quitting. What will he do when he realizes I'm gone?"

"He'll get a dose of his own medicine," Ike said.

"Should we call him?" Theo asked.

"He doesn't use a cell phone," April said. "Says it makes it too easy for people to find him. I should've left a note or something."

They thought about this for a few miles. Ike seemed refreshed and not at all sleepy. April's voice was stronger and she was over the shock.

"What about that Zack creep?" Theo asked. "Could we call him?"

"I don't know his number."

"What's his last name?" Ike asked.

"I don't know that either. I tried to keep my distance from Zack."

Another mile or two passed. Ike knocked back some coffee and said, "Here's what'll happen. When they can't find you, Zack will replay the story of seeing you with us.

He'll try and remember our names—Jack and Max Ford, formerly of Strattenburg but now living in Chapel Hill— and if he can, then they'll scramble around trying to find our phone number. When they can't find us, they'll assume you're at our house. Just old friends catching up after all these years."

"That's a stretch," April said.

"It's the best I can do."

"I should've left a note."

"Are you really that worried about your father?" Theo asked. "Look at what this guy did. He took you away in the middle of the night, didn't tell a single person, and for the past four days, the entire town has been worried sick. Your poor mother is out of her mind. I don't have much sympathy for him, April."

"I've never liked him," she said. "But I should've left a note."

"Too late," Ike said.

"They found a body on Thursday," Theo said, "and the whole town thought you were dead."

"A body?" she said.

Ike looked at Theo, and Theo looked at Ike, and away they went. Theo began with the story about their search party roaming through Strattenburg, passing out flyers, offering a reward, poking around empty buildings, dodging the police, and, finally, watching from across the river as the police pulled someone from the Yancey River. Ike added a few details here and there.

Theo said, "We thought you were dead, April. Left floating in the river by Jack Leeper. Mrs. Gladwell called us into assembly to try and cheer us up, but we knew you were dead."

"I'm so sorry."

"It's not your fault," Ike said. "Blame your father."

Theo turned around, looked at her, and said, "It's really good to see you, April."

Ike smiled to himself. His coffee cup was empty. They left North Carolina, crossed into Virginia, and Ike stopped for more coffee.

A few minutes after 2:00 a.m., Ike's cell phone vibrated. He fished it out of a pocket and said hello. It was his brother, Woods Boone, calling to chat. He and Mrs. Boone had just arrived home in Strattenburg, and they wanted an update on the road trip. Both kids were asleep, as was the dog, and Ike spoke softly. They were making good time; there was no traffic, no weather, and so far, no radar. Not surprisingly, Theo's parents were extremely curious about how he found April. Marcella picked up on another phone, and Ike told the story of Theo and Chase Whipple playing detectives, tracking down the band—with a bit of Ike's help—then randomly poring over thousands of Facebook photos until they got lucky. Once they confirmed the band was in the area, they started calling fraternities and sororities, and got lucky again.

Ike assured them April was fine. He relayed her version of all the lies her father had told her.

Theo's parents were still in disbelief, but also amused. And they were not really surprised that Theo had not only found April, but went to get her.

When the conversation was over, Ike shifted his weight, tried to stretch his right leg, wiggled here and there in his seat, and then, suddenly, almost fell asleep. "That's it!" he yelled. "Wake up, you two!" He punched Theo on the left shoulder, ruffled his hair, and said at high volume, "I almost ran off the road. You guys want to die? No! Theo, wake up and talk to me. April, it's your turn. Tell us a story."

April was rubbing her eyes, trying to wake up and understand why this crazy man was yelling at them. Even Judge looked confused.

At that moment, Ike hit the brakes and came to an abrupt stop on the shoulder of the road. He jumped out of the SUV and jogged around it three times. An 18-wheeler honked as it roared by. Ike got in, yanked his seat belt into place, then took off.

"April," he said loudly, "talk to me. I want to know exactly what happened when you left with your father."

"Sure, Ike," she said, afraid not to tell the story. "I was asleep," she began.

"Tuesday night or Wednesday morning?" Ike asked. "What time was it?"

"I don't know. It was after midnight because I was still awake at midnight. Then I fell asleep."

"Your mother was not there?" Theo asked.

"No, she was not. I talked to you on the phone, waited and waited for her to come home, then fell asleep. Someone was banging on my door. At first I thought it was a dream, another nightmare, but then I realized it wasn't, and this was even more terrifying. Someone was in the house, a man, banging on my door and calling my name. I was so scared I couldn't think, I couldn't see, I couldn't move. Then I realized it was my father. He was home, for the first time in a week. I opened the door. He asked where my mother was. I said I didn't know. She had not been home the last two or three nights. He started cursing, and he told me to change clothes. We were leaving. Hurry up. And so we left. As we drove away, I thought to myself—Leaving is better than staying. I'd rather be in the car with my father than in the house all alone."

She paused for a second. Ike was wide awake, as was Theo. Both wanted to look back and see if she was crying, but they did not.

"We drove for awhile, maybe two hours. I think we were close to D.C. when we stopped at a motel next to the interstate. We spent the night there, in the same room. When I woke up, he was gone. I waited. He came back with Egg McMuffins and orange juice. While we were eating, he told me he had found my mother, had a long talk with her, and she had agreed that it would be better for me if I stayed with him for a few days, maybe a week, maybe longer. She admitted, according to him, that she was having some problems and needed help. He told me that he had spoken to the principal at the school and she had agreed it would be wise if I stayed away from home. She would help me get extra tutoring if I needed it when I returned. I asked him the name of the principal, and, of course, he didn't know it. I remember thinking how odd, but then it would not be unusual for my father to forget someone's name ten seconds after a conversation with her."

Theo glanced back. April was gazing out the side window, seeing nothing, just chatting pleasantly with an odd smile on her face.

"We left that motel and drove to Charlottesville,

Virginia. The band played that night—Wednesday, I guess it was—at a place called Miller's. It's an old bar that's now famous because it's where the Dave Matthews Band got its start."

"I love that band," Theo said.

"They're okay," Ike said, a wiser voice from an older generation.

"My father thought it was so cool playing at Miller's."

"How'd you get in the bar when you're thirteen years old?" Theo asked.

"I don't know. I was with the band. It's not like I was drinking and smoking. The next day we drove to another town, maybe it was Roanoke, where the band played to an empty house in an old music hall. What day was that?"

"Thursday," Ike said.

"Then we drove to Raleigh."

"Were you in the van with the band?" Ike asked.

"No. My father had his car, as did two other guys. We always followed the van. Zack was the driver and the roadie. My father kept me away from the other band members. These guys fight and bicker worse than a bunch of little kids."

"And drugs?" Ike asked.

"Yes, and drinking, and girls. It's silly and kinda sad to

watch forty-year-old men trying to act cool in front of a bunch of college girls. But not my father. He was by far the best behaved."

"That's because you were around," Ike said.

"I suppose."

"How about a pit stop, Ike?" Theo said, pointing to a busy exit ahead.

"Sure. I need some more coffee."

"Where are we going when we get to Strattenburg?" April asked.

"Where do you want to go?" Ike asked.

"I'm not sure I want to go to my house," she said.

"Let's go to Theo's. His mother is trying to find your mother. I suspect she'll be there, and she'll be thrilled to see you."

# Chapter 21

There were some additional cars in the Boone driveway when Ike rolled up at ten minutes after 6:00 a.m. on Sunday morning. His old Spitfire was right where he'd left it. Beside it was a black sedan, very official looking. And behind the Spitfire was the strangest car in town—a bright-yellow hearse once owned by a funeral home but now the property of May Finnemore.

"She's here," April said. Neither Ike nor Theo could tell if this pleased her or not.

It was still dark when they parked. Judge leaped from the vehicle and ran to the holly bushes beside the porch, his favorite place to relieve himself. The front door flew open, and May Finnemore came sprinting out, already crying and reaching for her daughter. They embraced in the front yard for a long time, and as they did so, Ike, Theo, and Judge eased inside. Theo got hugged by his mother, then said hello to Detective Slater, who'd obviously been invited to join the party. After all the greetings and congratulations, Theo asked his mother, "Where did you find Mrs. Finnemore?"

"She was at a neighbor's house," Detective Slater said. "I knew about it. She's been too afraid to stay at home."

What about leaving April home alone, Theo almost blurted.

"Any word from Tom Finnemore?" Ike asked. "We left in a hurry and did not leave a note."

"Nothing," replied the detective.

"No surprise there."

"You must be exhausted," Mrs. Boone said.

Ike smiled and said, "Well, as a matter of fact, the answer is yes. And quite hungry. Theo and I have just spent the past fourteen hours on the road, with little to eat and no sleep, at least for me. Theo and April managed to nap a bit. The dog, though, slept for hours. What's for breakfast?"

"Everything," Mrs. Boone said.

"How'd you find her, Theo?" Mr. Boone asked, unable to conceal his pride.

"It's a long story, Dad, and I gotta use the restroom first." Theo disappeared and the front door opened. Mrs.

Finnemore and April entered, both in tears, both smiling. Mrs. Boone could not restrain herself and gave April a long hug. "We're so happy you're back," she said.

Detective Slater introduced himself to April, who was exhausted and unsettled and a little embarrassed by all the attention. "It's great to see you, kid," Slater said.

"Thank you," April said softly.

"Look, we can talk later," the detective said as he faced Mrs. Finnemore. "But I need to spend about five minutes with her right now."

"Can't this wait?" demanded Mrs. Boone, taking a step closer to April.

"Of course it can, Mrs. Boone. Except for one small matter that I need to explore now. After that, I'll get out of here and leave you alone."

"No one is asking you to leave, Detective," Mr. Boone said.

"I understand. Just give me five minutes."

Theo returned, and the Boones left the den and headed for the kitchen, where the thick smell of sausage hung in the air. Mrs. Finnemore and April sat on the sofa and the detective pulled a chair close.

He spoke in a low voice. "April, we're thrilled that you're back home, safe and sound. We're looking at the possibility of kidnapping charges. I've discussed it with your mother, and I need to ask you a couple of questions."

"Okay," she said timidly.

"First, when you left with your father, did you agree to do so? Did he force you to leave?"

April looked confused. She glanced at her mother, but her mother was staring at her boots.

Slater continued: "Kidnapping requires evidence that the victim was forced to leave against her will."

April slowly shook her head and said, "I was not forced to leave. I wanted to leave. I was very frightened."

Slater took a deep breath and looked at May, who was still avoiding all eye contact. "All right," he said. "The second question—Were you held against your will? Did you want to leave at any time, but were told you could not do so? With kidnapping, there are rare cases where a victim went away without objection, without force, sort of voluntarily, but then as time passed the victim changed her mind and wanted to go home. But her captor refused. At that point, it became a kidnapping. Is this what happened?"

April crossed her arms over her chest, gritted her teeth, and said, "No. That did not happen to me. My father was lying the whole time. He convinced me that he was in contact with my mother, that things were all right here, and that we would come home. Eventually. He never said when, but it would not be long. I never thought about running away, but I certainly could have. I wasn't guarded or locked up."

Another deep breath by the detective as his case continued to slip away. "One last question," he said. "Were you harmed in any way?"

"By my father? No. He might be a liar and a creep and a lousy father, but he would never harm me, nor would he let anyone else. I never felt threatened. I felt alone, and scared and confused, but that's not unusual for me even here in Strattenburg."

"April," Mrs. Finnemore said softly.

Detective Slater stood and said, "This will not be a criminal matter. It should be dealt with in the civil courts." He walked into the kitchen, thanked all the Boones there, and left. After he was gone, April and her mother joined the Boones around the kitchen table for a hearty breakfast of sausage, pancakes, and scrambled eggs. After the plates were served, the food properly blessed, and everyone had taken a bite or two, Ike said, "Slater couldn't wait to get out of here because he's too embarrassed. The police spent four days playing games with Leeper, and Theo solved the case in about two hours."

"How'd you do it, Theo?" his father demanded. "And I want the details."

"Let's hear it," his mother piped in.

Theo swallowed some eggs and looked around the table. Everyone was looking at him. He smiled, at first a nasty little grin, then a full-blown, ear-to-ear blast of orthodontic metal that was instantly contagious. April, already beyond braces, flashed a beautiful smile.

Unable to suppress it, Theo started laughing.


Detective Slater drove straight to the jail where he met Detective Capshaw. Together they waited in a small holding room while Jack Leeper was startled from his sleep, handcuffed, and practically dragged down the hall in his orange jumpsuit and orange rubber shower shoes. Two deputies hauled him into the holding room and sat him down in a metal chair. The handcuffs were not removed.

Leeper, his eyes still swollen and his face unshaven, looked at Slater and Capshaw and said, "Good morning. You boys are up mighty early."

"Where's the girl, Leeper?" Slater growled.

"Well, well, so you're back. You boys ready to make a deal this time?"

"Yep. We got a deal, a really good deal for you, Leeper.

But first you gotta tell us how far away the girl is. Just give us some idea. Five miles, fifty, five hundred?"

Leeper smiled at this. He rubbed his beard on his sleeve, grinned, and said, "She's about a hundred miles away."

Slater and Capshaw laughed.

"I say something funny?"

"You're such a lying scumbag, Leeper," Slater said. "I guess you'll lie all the way to your grave."

Capshaw took a step forward and said, "The girl's home with her momma, Leeper. Seems she took off with her father and spent a few days on the run. Now she's back, safe and sound. Thank God she never met you."

"You want a deal, Leeper?" Slater said. "Here's your deal. We're dropping all charges here, and we're gonna speed up your shipment back to California. We've talked to the authorities there and they've got a special place for you, as an escapee. Maximum security. You'll never see daylight."

Leeper's mouth opened but no words came out.

Slater said to the deputies, "Take him back." Then he and Capshaw left the room.


At 9:00 a.m., Sunday morning, the Strattenburg Police Department issued a statement to the press. It read: "At approximately six o'clock this morning, April Finnemore returned to Strattenburg and was reunited with her mother. She is safe, healthy, in good spirits, and was not harmed in any way. We are continuing our investigation into this matter and will interrogate her father, Tom Finnemore, as soon as possible."

The news was instantly broadcast on television and radio. It roared through the Internet. At dozens of churches, announcements were made to applause and thanksgiving.

The entire town took a deep breath, smiled, and thanked God for a miracle.

April missed it all. She was sound asleep in a small bedroom where the Boones sometimes kept their guests. She did not want to go home, at least not for a few hours. A neighbor called May Finnemore and relayed the news that their home was under siege from reporters, and said it would be wise to stay away until the mob left. Woods Boone suggested that she park her ridiculous vehicle in their garage; otherwise, someone would likely see it and know precisely where April was hiding.

Theo and Judge took a long nap in their upstairs bedroom.

## Chapter 22

When the students at Strattenburg Middle School returned to class on Monday morning, they expected a little excitement. This would not be a typical Monday. A dark cloud had hung over the school since April's disappearance, and now it was gone. Just a few days earlier everyone presumed her dead. Now she was back, and not only had she been found, she'd been rescued by one of their own. Theo's daring mission to Chapel Hill to pluck her from her father's captivity was quickly becoming a legend.

The arriving students were not disappointed. Before daybreak, half a dozen television vans were parked haphazardly around the wide, circular drive at the entrance of the school. Reporters were all over the place, with photographers waiting for a glimpse of something. This upset Mrs. Gladwell, and she called the police. A confrontation took place; angry words were exchanged; arrests were threatened. The police eventually moved the mob off school property, so the cameras were set up across the street. As this was happening, the buses began arriving and the students witnessed some of the conflict.

The bell rang at 8:15 for homeroom, but there was no sign of Theo and April. In Mr. Mount's room, Chase Whipple briefed the class on his participation in the search and rescue, which was received with rapt attention. On his Facebook page, Theo had posted a short version of what happened, and he gave plenty of credit to Chase.

At 8:30, Mrs. Gladwell again called all eighth graders to assembly. As they filed in, the mood was in stark contrast to the last gathering. Now the kids were lighthearted, laughing, and anxious to see April and forget this experience. Theo and April sneaked into the rear of the school, met Mr. Mount near the cafeteria, and hustled to assembly where they were mobbed by their classmates and hugged by their teachers.

April was anxious and obviously uncomfortable with the attention.

For Theo, though, it was his finest hour.

———

Later that morning, Marcella Boone appeared in Family Court to file a petition asking for the appointment of a temporary legal guardian for April Finnemore. Such a petition could be filed by any person concerned about the safety and well-being of any child. There was no requirement that notice be given to the child or to its parents when the petition was filed, but a temporary guardian would not be appointed unless good cause was shown to the court.

The judge was a large old man with a head full of curly white hair and a white beard and round, rosy cheeks that reminded a lot of people of Santa Claus. His name was Judge Jolly. In spite of his name, he was pious and strict, and because of this, and because of his appearance, he was known, behind his back all over town, as St. Nick.

He reviewed the petition while sitting on the bench, then asked Mrs. Boone, "Any sign of Tom Finnemore?"

Mrs. Boone had spent most of her career in Family Court, and knew St. Nick extremely well. She said, "I have been told that he called his wife last night and they talked for the first time in weeks. Supposedly, he will return home this afternoon."

"And no criminal charges are expected?"

"The police are treating this as a civil matter, not a criminal one."

"Do you have a recommendation as to who I should appoint as temporary guardian?"

"I do."

"Who?"

"Me."

"You're asking to be appointed?"

"That's correct, Your Honor. I know this situation very well. I know this child, her mother, and, to a much lesser extent, her father. I'm very concerned about what will happen to April, and I'm willing to serve as her temporary guardian for no fee."

"That's a good deal for everyone, Mrs. Boone," St. Nick said with a rare smile. "You are hereby appointed. What's your plan?"

"I would like to have an immediate hearing before this Court as soon as possible to determine where April should live for the next few days."

"Granted. When?"

"As soon as possible, Your Honor. If Mr. Finnemore returns today, I'll make sure he is immediately notified of the hearing."

"How about 9:00 a.m. tomorrow?"

"Perfect."

————

Tom Finnemore arrived home late Monday afternoon. Plunder's tour was over, and so was the band itself. The members had quarreled almost nonstop for two weeks, and they made little money. And they felt as though Tom had dragged them into his family mess by snatching his daughter and keeping her with him. April was just one of the many things they had fought over. Their biggest problem was that they were all middle-aged now, and too old to be playing for peanuts in frat houses and beer halls.

At home, Tom was met by his wife, who said little, and his daughter, who said even less. The women were united in their opposition to his presence, but Tom was too tired to fight. He went to the basement and locked the door. An hour later, a deputy arrived and handed him a summons to court. First thing in the morning.

# Chapter 23

After a few hours of tense negotiations, it was finally decided that Theo could skip school Tuesday morning and go to court. At first his parents said no way, but it became apparent that Theo was not about to back down. April was his friend. He knew a lot about her family. He had indeed rescued her, something he reminded his parents of several times. She might need his support, and so on. Mr. and Mrs. Boone finally got tired of arguing and said yes. But his father warned him about his homework, and his mother warned him that he would not be allowed inside the courtroom. In Family Court, matters dealing with children were always handled behind locked doors.

Theo thought he knew a way around this, and he had

a backup plan in the event St. Nick tossed him out of the courtroom.

The tossing happened rather fast.

In Family Court, all issues were decided by the judges, either St. Nick or Judge Judy Ping. (Ping-Pong as she was known, again behind her back. Most of the judges in the Stratten County Courthouse had a nickname or two.) There were no juries, and very few spectators. Therefore, the two courtrooms used for divorce trials, child custody disputes, adoptions, and dozens of other cases were much smaller than the courtrooms where juries were used and crowds gathered. And it was not unusual for the atmosphere to be tense when Family Court was called to order.

It was indeed tense on Tuesday morning. Theo and Mrs. Boone arrived early, and she allowed him to sit at her table as they waited. She pored over documents while Theo caught up on important matters with his laptop. The three Finnemores entered together. Mr. Gooch, one of an army of old semi-retired deputies who killed time in court as uniformed bailiffs, directed Tom Finnemore to his table on the left side of the room. May Finnemore was sent to hers on the right side of the room. April sat with Mrs. Boone in the center, directly in front of the judge's bench.

Theo thought it was a good sign that the family had arrived together. He would find out later that April rode her bike; her mother drove her yellow hearse, minus the monkey; and her father walked, for the exercise. They met at the front door of the courthouse and came in together.

Down the hall in Criminal Court, Judge Henry Gantry preferred the traditional, somewhat dramatic entry in which the bailiff makes everyone jump to their feet while he barks out, "All rise for the Court!" and so on, as the judge enters with his black robe flowing behind him. Theo preferred this, too, if only for the showmanship. There was an excellent chance he would one day become a great judge, much like Henry Gantry, and he certainly planned to stick to the more formal opening of court.

In what other job can an entire room of people, regardless of their age, job, or education, be required to stand in solemn respect as you enter the room? Theo could think of only three—queen of England, president of the United States, and judge.

St. Nick cared little for formalities. He walked in through a side door, followed by the clerk. He stepped up to the bench, took his seat in a battered leather rocker, and looked around the room. "Good morning," he said gruffly. There were a few mumbled replies.

"Tom Finnemore, I presume?" he asked, looking at April's father.

Mr. Finnemore stood nonchalantly and said, "That's me."

"Welcome home."

"Do I need a lawyer?"

"Keep your seat, sir. No, you do not need a lawyer. Maybe later." Mr. Finnemore sat down with a smirk. Theo looked at him and tried to remember him from the frenzy of the frat party last Saturday night. He was the band's drummer and had been partially hidden by the tools of his trade. He sort of looked familiar, but then Theo had not had the time to examine Plunder. Tom Finnemore was a nice-looking man, respectable in some ways. He was wearing cowboy boots and jeans, but his sports coat was stylish.

"And you are May Finnemore?" St. Nick asked, nodding to the right.

"Yes, sir."

"And Mrs. Boone, you are with April?"

"Yes, sir."

St. Nick glared down at Theo for a few seconds, then said, "Theo, what are you doing here?"

"April asked me to be here."

"Oh, she did? Are you a witness?"

"I could be."

St. Nick managed a smile. His reading glasses were perched far down at the end of his nose, and when he smiled, which didn't happen often, his eyes twinkled and he did in fact resemble Santa Claus. "You could also be a lawyer, a bailiff, or a clerk, couldn't you, Theo?"

"I suppose."

"You could also be the judge and decide this matter, couldn't you?"

"Probably."

"Mrs. Boone, is there any legitimate reason for your son to be in this courtroom during this hearing?"

"Not really," Mrs. Boone said.

"Theo, go to school."

The bailiff stepped toward Theo and gently waved an arm toward the door. Theo grabbed his backpack and said, "Thanks, Mom." He whispered to April, "See you at school," and then took off.

However, he had no plans to go to school. He left his backpack on a bench outside the courtroom, ran downstairs to the snack bar, bought a large root beer in a paper cup, ran back up the stairs, and, when no one was looking, dropped the drink onto the shiny marble floor. Ice and root beer splashed and ran into a wide circle. Theo did not slow down. He jogged down the hall, past Family Court, around a corner to a small room that served as a utility closet, storage area, and napping place of Mr. Speedy Cobb, the oldest and slowest janitor in the history of Stratten County. As expected, Speedy was resting, catching a quick nap before the rigors of the day kicked in.

"Speedy, I dropped a drink down the hall. It's a mess!" Theo said urgently.

"Hello, Theo. What are you doing here?" The same question every time he saw Theo. Speedy was getting to his feet, grabbing a mop.

"Just hanging out. I'm really sorry about this," Theo said.

With a mop and a bucket, Speedy eventually made it down the hall. He scratched his chin and inspected the spill as if the operation would take hours and require great skill. Theo watched him for a few seconds, and then retreated to Speedy's little room. The cramped and dirty place where Speedy napped was next to a slightly larger room where supplies were stored. Quickly, Theo climbed up the shelves, passing rows of paper towels, toilet paper, and sanitizer. Above the top shelf was a crawl space, dark and narrow with an air vent to one side. Below the air vent, some fifteen feet away, was the desk of St. Nick himself. From his secret cubbyhole, known only to himself, Theo could see nothing.

But he could hear every word.

# Chapter 24

St. Nick was saying, "The issue before this Court is the temporary placement of April Finnemore. Not legal custody, but placement. I have a preliminary report from Social Services that recommends that April be placed in foster care until other matters can be resolved. Those other matters might, and I repeat the word *might*, include divorce proceedings, criminal charges against the father, psychiatric evaluations of both parents, and so on. We cannot anticipate all of the legal battles that lie ahead. My job today is to decide where to place April while her parents attempt to bring some order to their lives. This preliminary report concludes with the belief that she is not safe at home. Mrs. Boone, have you had time to read the report?"

"Yes, Your Honor."

"Do you agree with it?"

"Yes and no, Your Honor. Last night, April was at home, with both parents in the house, and she felt safe. The night before, she was at home with her mother, and she felt safe. But last week, on Monday night and Tuesday night, she was at home alone and had no idea where either parent was. Around midnight Tuesday, her father showed up, and because she was terrified, she left with him. Now, we all know the rest of the story. April wants to be at home with her parents, but I'm not sure her parents want to be home with her. Perhaps, Your Honor, we should hear from her parents."

"Precisely. Mr. Finnemore, what are your plans for the near future? Do you plan to stay at home, or leave? Tour again with your rock band, or finally give it up? Get a job, or continue to drift here and there? File for divorce, or get some professional help? A clue here, Mr. Finnemore. Give us some idea of what we can expect from you."

Tom Finnemore hunkered down under the barrage of loaded questions suddenly aimed at him. For a long time, he said nothing. Everyone waited and waited and after a while it appeared as though he had no response. But when he spoke, his voice was scratchy, almost cracking. "I don't know, Judge. I just don't know. I took April last week because she was scared to death and we had no idea where May was. After we left, I called several times, never got an answer, and as time passed I guess I quit calling. It never occurred to me that the whole town would think she had been kidnapped and murdered. It was a big mistake on my part. I'm really sorry."

He wiped his eyes, cleared his throat, and continued: "I think the rock tours are over, kind of a dead-end road, you know. To answer your question, Judge, I plan to be at home a lot more. I'd like to spend more time with April, but I'm not sure about spending time with her mother."

"Have the two of you discussed a divorce?"

"Judge, we've been married for twenty-four years, and we separated the first time after two months of marriage. Divorce has always been a hot topic."

"What's your response to the report's conclusion that April be removed from your home and placed somewhere safe?"

"Please don't do that, sir. I'll stay home, I promise. I'm not sure what May will do, but I can promise this Court that one of us will be at home for April."

"That sounds good, Mr. Finnemore, but, frankly, you don't have a lot of credibility with me right now."

"I know, Judge, and I understand. But, please don't take

her away." He wiped his eyes again and went silent. St. Nick waited, then turned to the other side of the room and said, "And you?"

May Finnemore had a tissue in both hands and looked as though she'd been crying for days. She mumbled and stammered before finding her voice. "It's not a great home, Judge; I guess that much is obvious. But it's our home; it's April's home. Her room is there, her clothes and books and things. Maybe her parents are not always there, but we'll do better. You can't take April out of her home and put her with strangers. Please don't do that."

"And your plans, Mrs. Finnemore? More of the same, or are you willing to change your ways?"

May Finnemore pulled papers out of a file and gave them to the bailiff, who in turn handed each one to the judge, Mr. Finnemore, and Mrs. Boone. "This is a letter from my therapist. He explains that I'm under his care now and that he is optimistic about my improvement."

Everyone read the letter. Though couched in medical terms, the bottom line was that May had emotional problems, and to deal with them she had gotten herself mixed up with various and unnamed prescription drugs. She continued, "He has enrolled me in a rehab program as an outpatient. I'm tested every morning at eight a.m."

"When did you start this program?" St. Nick asked.

"Last week. I went to see the therapist after April disappeared. I'm much better already, I promise, Your Honor."

St. Nick put the letter down and looked at April. "I'd like to hear from you," he said with a warm smile. "What are your thoughts, April? What do you want?"

In a voice much stronger than either parent, April began, "Well, Judge, what I want is something that's impossible. I want what every kid wants—a normal home and a normal family. But that is not what I have. We don't do normal, and I've learned to live with that. My brother and sister learned to live with it. They left home as soon as possible, and they're doing okay out in the world. They survived, and I'll survive, too, if I can have a little help. I want a father who doesn't leave for a month without saying good-bye and without calling home. I want a mother who'll protect me. I can deal with a lot of the crazy stuff, as long as they don't run away." Her voice began to break, but she was determined to finish. "I'm leaving, too, as soon as I can. Until then, though, please don't abandon me."

She looked at her father and saw nothing but tears. She looked at her mother and saw the same.

St. Nick looked at the lawyer and said, "As April's guardian, Mrs. Boone, do you have a recommendation?"

"I have a recommendation, Your Honor, and I have a plan," Marcella Boone said.

"I'm not surprised. Continue."

"My recommendation is that April remain at home tonight and tomorrow night, and then on a nightly basis. If either parent plans to be away from home during the night, that parent must notify me in advance, and I'll notify the Court. Further, I recommend the parents begin marriage counseling immediately. I suggest Doctor Francine Street, who is in my opinion the best in town. I've taken the liberty of setting up an appointment this afternoon at five p.m. Doctor Street will keep me posted on the progress. If either parent fails to show up for counseling, then I will be notified immediately. I will contact Mrs. Finnemore's new therapist and ask to be updated on her progress in rehab."

St. Nick stroked his beard and nodded at Mrs. Boone. "I like it," he said. "What about you, Mr. Finnemore?"

"Sounds reasonable, Your Honor."

"And you, Mrs. Finnemore?"

"I'll agree to anything, Judge. Just please don't take her away."

"Then it is so ordered. Anything else, Mrs. Boone?"

"Yes, Your Honor. I have arranged for April to have a cell phone. If something happens, if she feels threatened or in danger, or whatever, then she can call me immediately. If for some reason I'm not available, she can call my paralegal, or perhaps someone with the Court. Plus, I'm sure she can always find Theo."

St. Nick thought for a second and smiled, then said, "And I'm sure Theo can always find her."

Fifteen feet above, in the dark intestines of the Stratten County Courthouse, Theodore Boone smiled to himself.

The hearing was over.

Speedy was back, shuffling through his cramped room below, mumbling to himself as he put his mop away and accidentally kicked his bucket. Theo was trapped and he really wanted to get out of the building and go to school. He waited. Minutes passed, then he heard the familiar sound of Speedy snoring, fast asleep as usual. Silently, Theo climbed down the shelves and landed on the floor. Speedy was kicked back in his favorite chair, cap pulled down over his eyes, mouth open, dead to the world. Theo eased by and made his escape. He was hustling down the wide hallway, almost to the sweeping staircase when he heard someone call his name. It was Judge Henry Gantry, Theo's favorite judge in the entire courthouse.

"Theo," he called loudly.

Theo stopped, turned, and began walking to the judge.

Henry Gantry was not smiling, though he seldom did. He was carrying a thick file of some sort and he was not wearing his black robe. "Why aren't you in school?" he demanded.

More than once, Theo had played hooky or skipped school to watch a trial, and on at least two occasions he'd been caught red-handed, in the courtroom. "I was in court with my mother," he said, somewhat truthfully. He was looking up. Judge Gantry was looking down.

"Would this have anything to do with the April Finnemore case?" he asked. Strattenburg was not a large city and there were few secrets, especially among the lawyers, judges, and police.

"Yes, sir."

"I hear you found the girl and brought her home," Judge Gantry said with the first hint of a smile.

"Something like that," Theo said modestly.

"Nice work, Theo."

"Thanks."

"Just so you'll know, I've rescheduled the Duffy trial to begin in six weeks. I'm sure you'll want front-row seats."

Theo could think of nothing to say. The first murder trial of Pete Duffy had been the biggest in the town's history, and, thanks to Theo, it had ended in a mistrial. The second promised to be even more suspenseful.

Theo finally said, "Sure, Judge."

"We'll talk about it later. Get to school."

"Sure thing." Theo bounded down the stairs, jumped on his bike, and raced away from the courthouse. He had a lunch date with April. They planned to meet outside the school cafeteria at noon and steal away to the old gym where no one could find them. Mrs. Boone had packed veggie sandwiches, April's favorite and Theo's least favorite, and peanut butter cookies.

Theo wanted to hear every last detail of the abduction.

Read where it all began . . .

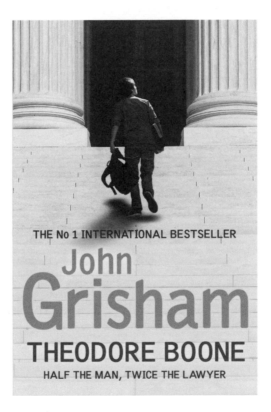

THE No 1 INTERNATIONAL BESTSELLER

John
Grisham

THEODORE BOONE
HALF THE MAN, TWICE THE LAWYER

HODDER &
STOUGHTON

# Chapter 1

Theodore Boone was an only child and for that reason usually had breakfast alone. His father, a busy lawyer, was in the habit of leaving early and meeting friends for coffee and gossip at the same downtown diner every morning at seven. Theo's mother, herself a busy lawyer, had been trying to lose ten pounds for at least the past ten years, and because of this she'd convinced herself that breakfast should be nothing more than coffee with the newspaper. So he ate by himself at the kitchen table, cold cereal and orange juice, with an eye on the clock. The Boone home had clocks everywhere, clear evidence of organized people.

Actually, he wasn't completely alone. Beside his chair, his dog ate, too. Judge was a thoroughly mixed mutt whose age and breeding would always be a mystery. Theo had rescued him from near death with a last-second appearance in Animal Court two years earlier, and Judge would always be grateful. He preferred Cheerios, same as Theo, and they ate together in silence every morning.

At 8:00 a.m., Theo rinsed their bowls in the sink, placed the milk and juice back in the fridge, walked to the den, and kissed his mother on the cheek. "Off to school," he said.

"Do you have lunch money?" she asked, the same question five mornings a week.

"Always."

"And your homework is complete?"

"It's perfect, Mom."

"And I'll see you when?"

"I'll stop by the office after school." Theo stopped by the office every day after school, without fail, but Mrs. Boone always asked.

"Be careful," she said. "And remember to smile." The braces on his teeth had now been in place for over two years and Theo wanted desperately to get rid of them. In the meantime, though, his mother continually reminded him to smile and make the world a happier place.

"I'm smiling, Mom."

"Love you, Teddy."

"Love you back."

Theo, still smiling in spite of being called "Teddy," flung his backpack across his shoulders, scratched Judge on the head and said good-bye, then left through the kitchen door. He hopped on his bike and was soon speeding down Mallard Lane, a narrow leafy street in the oldest section of town. He waved at Mr. Nunnery, who was already on his porch and settled in for another long day of watching what little traffic found its way into their neighborhood, and he whisked by Mrs. Goodloe at the curb without speaking because she'd lost her hearing and most of her mind as well. He did smile at her, though, but she did not return the smile. Her teeth were somewhere in the house.

It was early spring and the air was crisp and cool. Theo pedaled quickly, the wind stinging his face. Homeroom was at eight forty and he had important matters before school. He cut through a side street, darted down an alley, dodged some traffic, and ran a stop sign. This was Theo's turf, the route he traveled every day. After four blocks the houses gave way to offices and shops and stores.

The county courthouse was the largest building in downtown Strattenburg (the post office was second, the library third). It sat majestically on the north side of Main Street, halfway between a bridge over the river and a park filled with gazebos and birdbaths and monuments to those killed in wars. Theo loved the courthouse, with its air of authority, and people hustling importantly about, and somber notices and schedules tacked to the bulletin boards. Most of all, Theo loved the courtrooms themselves. There were small ones where more private matters were handled without juries, then there was the main courtroom on the second floor where lawyers battled like gladiators and judges ruled like kings.

At the age of thirteen, Theo was still undecided about his future. One day he dreamed of being a famous trial lawyer, one who handled the biggest cases and never lost before juries. The next day he dreamed of being a great judge, noted for his wisdom and fairness. He went back and forth, changing his mind daily.

The main lobby was already busy on this Monday morning, as if the lawyers and their clients wanted an early start to the week. There was a crowd waiting by the elevator, so Theo raced up two flights of stairs and down the east wing where Family Court was held. His mother was a noted divorce lawyer, one who always represented the wife, and Theo knew this area of the building well. Since divorce trials were decided by judges, juries were not used, and since most judges preferred not to have large groups of spectators observing such sensitive matters, the courtroom was small. By its door, several lawyers huddled importantly, obviously not agreeing on much. Theo searched the hallway, then turned a corner and saw his friend.

She was sitting on one of the old wooden benches, alone, small and frail and nervous. When she saw him she smiled and put a hand over her mouth. Theo hustled over and sat next to her, very closely, knees touching. With any other girl he would have placed himself at least two feet away and prevented any chance of contact.

But April Finnemore was not just any girl. They had started prekindergarten together at the age of four at a nearby church school, and they had been close friends since they could remember. It wasn't a romance; they were too young for that. Theo did not know of a single thirteen-year-old boy in his class who admitted to having a girlfriend. Just the opposite. They wanted nothing to do with them. And the girls felt the same way. Theo had been warned that things would change, and dramatically, but that seemed unlikely.

April was just a friend, and one in a great deal of need at the moment. Her parents were divorcing, and Theo was extremely grateful his mother was not involved with the case.

The divorce was no surprise to anyone who knew the Finnemores. April's father was an eccentric antiques dealer and the drummer for an old rock band that still played in nightclubs and toured for weeks at a time. Her mother raised goats and made goat cheese, which she peddled around town in a converted funeral hearse, painted bright yellow. An ancient spider monkey with gray whiskers rode shotgun and munched on the cheese, which had never sold very well. Mr. Boone had once described the family as "nontraditional," which Theo took to mean downright weird. Both her parents had been arrested on drug charges, though neither had served time.

"Are you okay?" Theo asked.

"No," she said. "I hate being here."

She had an older brother named August and an older sister named March, and both fled the family. August left the day after he graduated from high school. March dropped out at the age of sixteen and left town, leaving April as the only child for her parents to torment. Theo knew all of this because April told him everything. She had to. She needed someone outside of her family to confide in, and Theo was her listener.

"I don't want to live with either one of them," she said. It was a terrible thing to say about one's parents, but Theo understood completely. He despised her parents for the way they treated her. He despised them for the chaos of their lives, for their neglect of April, for their cruelty to her. Theo had a long list of grudges against Mr. and Mrs. Finnemore. He would run away before being forced to live there. He did not know of a single kid in town who'd ever set foot inside the Finnemore home.

The divorce trial was in its third day, and April would soon be called to the witness stand to testify. The judge would ask her the fateful question, "April, which parent do you want to live with?"

And she did not know the answer. She had discussed it for hours with Theo, and she still did not know what to say.

The great question in Theo's mind was, "Why did either parent want custody of April?" Each had neglected her in so many ways. He had heard many stories, but he had never repeated a single one.

"What are you going to say?" he asked.

"I'm telling the judge that I want to live with my aunt Peg in Denver."

"I thought she said no."

"She did."

"Then you can't say that."

"What can I say, Theo?"

"My mother would say that you should choose your mother. I know she's not your first choice, but you don't have a first choice."

"But the judge can do whatever he wants, right?"

"Right. If you were fourteen, you could make a binding decision. At thirteen, the judge will only consider your wishes. According to my mother, this judge almost never awards custody to the father. Play it safe. Go with your mother."

April wore jeans, hiking boots, and a navy sweater. She rarely dressed like a girl, but her gender was never in doubt. She wiped a tear from her cheek, but managed to keep her composure. "Thanks, Theo," she said.

"I wish I could stay."

"And I wish I could go to school."

They both managed a forced laugh. "I'll be thinking about you. Be strong."

"Thanks, Theo."

His favorite judge was the Honorable Henry Gantry, and he entered the great man's outer office at twenty minutes after 8:00 a.m.

"Well, good morning, Theo," Mrs. Hardy said. She was stirring something into her coffee and preparing to begin her work.

"Morning, Mrs. Hardy," Theo said with a smile.

"And to what do we owe this honor?" she asked. She

was not quite as old as Theo's mother, he guessed, and she was very pretty. She was Theo's favorite of all the secretaries in the courthouse. His favorite clerk was Jenny over in Family Court.

"I need to see Judge Gantry," he replied. "Is he in?"

"Well, yes, but he's very busy."

"Please. It'll just take a minute."

She sipped her coffee, then asked, "Does this have anything to do with the big trial tomorrow?"

"Yes, ma'am, it does. I'd like for my Government class to watch the first day of the trial, but I gotta make sure there will be enough seats."

"Oh, I don't know about that, Theo," Mrs. Hardy said, frowning and shaking her head. "We're expecting an overflow crowd. Seating will be tight."

"Can I talk to the judge?"

"How many are in your class?"

"Sixteen. I thought maybe we could sit in the balcony."

She was still frowning as she picked up the phone and pushed a button. She waited for a second, then said, "Yes, Judge, Theodore Boone is here and would like to see you. I told him you are very busy." She listened some more, then put down the phone. "Hurry," she said, pointing to the judge's door.

Seconds later, Theo stood before the biggest desk in town,

a desk covered with all sorts of papers and files and thick binders, a desk that symbolized the enormous power held by Judge Henry Gantry, who, at that moment, was not smiling. In fact, Theo was certain the judge had not cracked a smile since he'd interrupted his work. Theo, though, was pressing hard with a prolonged flash of metal from ear to ear.

"State your case," Judge Gantry said. Theo had heard him issue this command on many occasions. He'd seen lawyers, good lawyers, rise and stutter and search for words while Judge Gantry scowled down from the bench. He wasn't scowling now, nor was he wearing his black robe, but he was still intimidating. As Theo cleared his throat, he saw an unmistakable twinkle in his friend's eye.

"Yes, sir, well, my Government teacher is Mr. Mount, and Mr. Mount thinks we might get approval from the principal for an all-day field trip to watch the opening of the trial tomorrow." Theo paused, took a deep breath, told himself again to speak clearly, slowly, forcefully, like all great trial lawyers. "But, we need guaranteed seats. I was thinking we could sit in the balcony."

"Oh, you were?"

"Yes, sir."

"How many?"

"Sixteen, plus Mr. Mount."

The judge picked up a file, opened it, and began reading

as if he'd suddenly forgotten about Theo standing at attention across the desk. Theo waited for an awkward fifteen seconds. Then the judge abruptly said, "Seventeen seats, front balcony, left side. I'll tell the bailiff to seat you at ten minutes before nine, tomorrow. I expect perfect behavior."

"No problem, sir."

"I'll have Mrs. Hardy e-mail a note to your principal."

"Thanks, Judge."

"You can go now, Theo. Sorry to be so busy."

"No problem, sir."

Theo was scurrying toward the door when the judge said, "Say, Theo. Do you think Mr. Duffy is guilty?"

Theo stopped, turned around and without hesitating responded, "He's presumed innocent."

"Got that. But what's your opinion as to his guilt?"

"I think he did it."

The judge nodded slightly but gave no indication of whether he agreed.

"What about you?" Theo asked.

Finally, a smile. "I'm a fair and impartial referee, Theo. I have no preconceived notions of guilt or innocence."

"That's what I thought you'd say."

"See you tomorrow." Theo cracked the door and hustled out.

Mrs. Hardy was on her feet, hands on hips, staring

down two flustered lawyers who were demanding to see the judge. All three clammed up when Theo walked out of Judge Gantry's office. He smiled at Mrs. Hardy as he walked hurriedly by. "Thanks," he said as he opened the door and disappeared.

# Chapter 2

The ride from the courthouse to the middle school would take fifteen minutes if properly done, if one obeyed the traffic laws and refrained from trespassing. And normally this is the way Theo would do things, except when he was running a bit late. He flew down Market Street the wrong way, jumped the curb just ahead of a car, and bolted through a parking lot, used every sidewalk available, then—his most serious offense—he ducked between two houses on Elm Street. Theo heard someone yelling from the porch behind him until he was safely into an alley that ran into the teachers' parking lot behind his school. He checked his watch—nine minutes. Not bad.

He parked at the rack by the flagpole, secured his bike with a chain, then entered with a flood of kids who'd just stepped off a bus. The eight forty bell was ringing when he walked into his homeroom and said good morning to Mr. Mount, who not only taught him Government but was his adviser as well.

"Talked to Judge Gantry," Theo said at the teacher's desk, one considerably smaller than the one he'd just left in the courthouse. The room was buzzing with the usual early morning chaos. All sixteen boys were present and all appeared to be involved in some sort of gag, scuffle, joke, or shoving match.

"And?"

"Got the seats, first thing in the morning."

"Excellent. Great job, Theo."

Mr. Mount eventually restored order, called the roll, made his announcements, and ten minutes later sent the boys down the hall to their first period Spanish class with Madame Monique. There was some awkward flirting between the rooms as the boys mixed with the girls. During classes, they were "gender-separated," according to a new policy adopted by the smart people in charge of educating all the children in town. The genders were free to mingle at all other times.

Madame Monique was a tall, dark lady from Cameroon, in West Africa. She had moved to Strattenburg three years earlier when her husband, also from Cameroon, took a job at the local college where he taught languages. She was not the typical teacher at the middle school, far from it. As a child in Africa, she had grown up speaking Beti, her tribal dialect, as well as French and English, the official languages of Cameroon. Her father was a doctor, and thus could afford to send her to school in Switzerland, where she picked up German and Italian. Her Spanish had been perfected when she went to college in Madrid. She was currently working on Russian with plans to move on to Mandarin Chinese. Her classroom was filled with large, colorful maps of the world, and her students believed she'd been everywhere, seen everything, and could speak any language. It's a big world, she told them many times, and most people in other countries speak more than one language. While the students concentrated on Spanish, they were also encouraged to explore others.

Theo's mother had been studying Spanish for twenty years, and as a preschooler he had learned from her many of the basic words and phrases. Some of her clients were from Central America, and when Theo saw them at the office he was ready to practice. They always thought it was cute.

Madame Monique had told him that he had an ear for

languages, and this had inspired him to study harder. She was often asked by her curious students to "say something in German." Or, "Speak some Italian." She would, but first the student making the request had to stand and say a few words in that language. Bonus points were given, and this created enthusiasm. Most of the boys in Theo's class knew a few dozen words in several languages. Aaron, who had a Spanish mother and a German father, was by far the most talented linguist. But Theo was determined to catch him. After Government, Spanish was his favorite class, and Madame Monique ran a close second to Mr. Mount as his favorite teacher.

Today, though, he had trouble concentrating. They were studying Spanish verbs, a tedious chore on a good day, and Theo's mind was elsewhere. He worried about April and her awful day on the witness stand. He couldn't imagine the horror of being forced to choose one parent over another. And when he managed to set April aside, he was consumed with the murder trial and couldn't wait until tomorrow, to watch the opening statements by the lawyers.

Most of his classmates dreamed of getting tickets to the big game or concert. Theo Boone lived for the big trials.


Second period was Geometry with Miss Garman. It was followed by a short break outdoors, then the class returned to homeroom, to Mr. Mount and the best hour of the day, at least in Theo's opinion. Mr. Mount was in his midthirties, and had once worked as a lawyer at a gigantic firm in a skyscraper in Chicago. His brother was a lawyer. His father and grandfather had been lawyers and judges. Mr. Mount, though, had grown weary of the long hours and high pressure, and, well, he'd quit. He'd walked away from the big money and found something he found far more rewarding. He loved teaching, and though he still thought of himself as a lawyer, he considered the classroom far more important than the courtroom.

Because he knew the law so well, his Government class spent most of its time discussing cases, old ones and current ones and even fictitious ones on television.

"All right, men," he began when they were seated and still. He always addressed them as "men" and for thirteen-year-olds there was no greater compliment. "Tomorrow I want you here at eight fifteen. We'll take a bus to the courthouse and we'll be in our seats in plenty of time. It's a field trip, approved by the principal, so you will be excused from all other classes. Bring lunch money and we'll eat at Pappy's Deli. Any questions?"

The men were hanging on every word, excitement all over their faces.

"What about backpacks?" someone asked.

"No," Mr. Mount answered. "You can't take anything into the courtroom. Security will be tight. It is, after all, the first murder trial here in a long time. Any more questions?"

"What should we wear?"

Slowly, all eyes turned to Theo, including those of Mr. Mount. It was well known that Theo spent more time in the courthouse than most lawyers.

"Coat and tie, Theo?" Mr. Mount asked.

"No, not at all. What we're wearing now is fine."

"Great. Any more questions? Good. Now, I've asked Theo if he would sort of set the stage for tomorrow. Lay out the courtroom, give us the players, tell us what we're in for. Theo."

Theo's laptop was already wired to the overhead projector. He walked to the front of the class, pressed a key, and a large diagram appeared on the digital wide-screen whiteboard. "This is the main courtroom," Theo said, in his best lawyer's voice. He held a laser pointer with a red light and sort of waved it around the diagram. "At the top, in the center here, is the bench. That's where the judge sits and controls the trial. Not sure why it's called a bench. It's more like a throne. But, anyway, we'll stick with bench. The judge is Henry Gantry." He punched a key, and a large formal photo of Judge Gantry appeared. Black robe, somber face. Theo shrank it, then dragged it up to the bench. With the judge in place, he continued, "Judge Gantry has been a judge for about twenty years and handles only criminal cases. He runs a tight courtroom and is well liked by most of the lawyers." The laser pointer moved to the middle of the courtroom. "This is the defense table, where Mr. Duffy, the man accused of murder, will be seated." Theo punched a key and a black-and-white photo, one taken from a newspaper, appeared. "This is Mr. Duffy. Age forty-nine, used to be married to Mrs. Duffy, who is now deceased, and as we all know, Mr. Duffy is accused of murdering her." He shrank the photo and moved it to the defense table. "His lawyer is Clifford Nance, probably the top criminal defense lawyer in this part of the state." Nance appeared in color, wearing a dark suit and a shifty smile. He had long, curly gray hair. His photo was reduced and placed next to his client's. "Next to the defense table is the prosecution's table. The lead prosecutor is Jack Hogan, who's also known as the district attorney, or DA." Hogan's photo appeared for a few seconds before it was reduced and placed at the table next to the defense.

"Where'd you find these photos?" someone asked.

"Each year the bar association publishes a directory of all the lawyers and judges," Theo answered.

"Are you included?" This brought a few light laughs.

"No. Now, there will be other lawyers and paralegals at both tables, prosecution and defense. This area is usually crowded. Over here, next to the defense, is the jury box. It has fourteen chairs—twelve for the jurors and two for the alternates. Most states still use twelve-man juries, though different sizes are not unusual. Regardless of the number, the verdict has to be unanimous, at least in criminal cases. They pick alternates in case one of the twelve gets sick or excused or something. The jury was selected last week, so we won't have to watch that. It's pretty boring." The laser pointer moved to a spot in front of the bench. Theo continued, "The court reporter sits here. She'll have a machine that is called a stenograph. Sorta looks like a typewriter, but much different. Her job is to record every word that's said during the trial. That might sound impossible, but she makes it look easy. Later, she'll prepare what's known as a transcript so that the lawyers and the judge will have a record of everything. Some transcripts have thousands of pages." The laser pointer moved again. "Here, close to the court reporter and just down from the judge, is the witness chair. Each witness walks up here, is sworn to tell the truth, then takes a seat."

"Where do we sit?"

The laser pointer moved to the middle of the diagram. "This is called the bar. Again, don't ask why. The bar is a wooden railing that separates the spectators from the trial area. There are ten rows of seats with an aisle down the middle. This is usually more than enough for the crowd, but this trial will be different." The laser pointer moved to the rear of the courtroom. "Up here, above the last few rows, is the balcony where there are three long benches. We're in the balcony, but don't worry. We'll be able to see and hear everything."

"Any questions?" Mr. Mount asked.

The boys gawked at the diagram. "Who goes first?" someone asked.

Theo began pacing. "Well, the State has the burden of proving guilt, so it must present its case first. First thing tomorrow morning, the prosecutor will walk to the jury box and address the jurors. This is called the opening statement. He'll lay out his case. Then the defense lawyer will do the same. After that, the State will start calling witnesses. As you know, Mr. Duffy is presumed to be innocent, so the State must prove him guilty, and it must do so beyond a reasonable doubt. He claims he's innocent, which actually in real life doesn't happen very often. About eighty percent of those indicted for murder eventually plead guilty, because they are in fact guilty. The other twenty percent go to trial, and ninety percent of those are found guilty. So, it's rare for a murder defendant to be found not guilty."

"My dad thinks he's guilty," Brian said.

"A lot of people do," Theo said.

"How many trials have you watched, Theo?"

"I don't know. Dozens."

Since none of the other fifteen had ever seen the inside of a courtroom, this was almost beyond belief. Theo continued: "For those of you who watch a lot of television, don't expect fireworks. A real trial is very different, and not nearly as exciting. There are no surprise witnesses, no dramatic confessions, no fistfights between the lawyers. And, in this trial, there are no eyewitnesses to the murder. This means that all of the evidence from the State will be circumstantial. You'll hear this word a lot, especially from Mr. Clifford Nance, the defense lawyer. He'll make a big deal out of the fact that the State has no direct proof, that everything is circumstantial."

"I'm not sure what that means," someone said.

"It means that the evidence is indirect, not direct. For example, did you ride your bike to school?"

"Yes."

"And did you chain it to the rack by the flagpole?"

"Yes."

"So, when you leave school this afternoon, and you go to the rack, and your bike is gone, and the chain has been cut, then you have indirect evidence that someone stole your bike. No one saw the thief, so there's no direct evidence. And let's say that tomorrow the police find your bike in a pawnshop on Raleigh Street, a place known to deal in stolen bikes. The owner gives the police a name, they investigate and find some dude with a history of stealing bikes. You can then make a strong case, through indirect evidence, that this guy is your thief. No direct evidence, but circumstantial."

Even Mr. Mount was nodding along. He was the faculty adviser for the Eighth-Grade Debate Team, and, not surprisingly, Theodore Boone was his star. He'd never had a student as quick on his feet.

"Thank you, Theo," Mr. Mount said. "And thank you for getting us the seats in the morning."

"Nothing to it," Theo said, and proudly took his seat.

It was a bright class in a strong public school. Justin was by far the best athlete, though he couldn't swim as fast as Brian. Ricardo beat them all at golf and tennis. Edward played the cello, Woody the electric guitar, Darren the drums, Jarvis the trumpet. Joey had the highest IQ and made perfect grades. Chase was the mad scientist who was always a threat to blow up the lab. Aaron spoke Spanish, from his mother's side, German from his father's, and English, of course. Brandon had an early morning paper route, traded stocks online, and planned to be the first millionaire in the group.

Naturally, there were two hopeless nerds and at least one potential felon.

The class even had its own lawyer, a first for Mr. Mount.